After spending two years away at culinary school, learning the arts of baking and magic, all Karl wants to do after graduation is return home to the kitchen where he grew up. However, when Karl's adoptive uncle asks him to do a little favor for him along his journey, of course Karl says yes. He needs to find a missing person, one who may have been captured somewhere in Yaroi, a neighboring country to Karl's home in Toval.

Finding the missing person is hard enough. Add in each of their secretive pasts, and the implications and dangers inherent with being a Prince of Toval, and a simple rescue turns into a deadly adventure. Especially once Karl learns just why Ama was arrested in the first place. Karl's chances of returning home to use his newly honed baking skills dwindle as escaping the situation with their heads still attached is proving to be almost impossible.

THE SPY

PRINCES OF TOVAL, BOOK THREE

MELL EIGHT

A NineStar Press Publication
www.ninestarpress.com

The Spy

First Edition, June 2025

ISBN: 978-1-64890-872-9

Also available in eBook, ISBN: 978-1-64890-871-2

CONTENT WARNING:

This book contains depictions of torture.

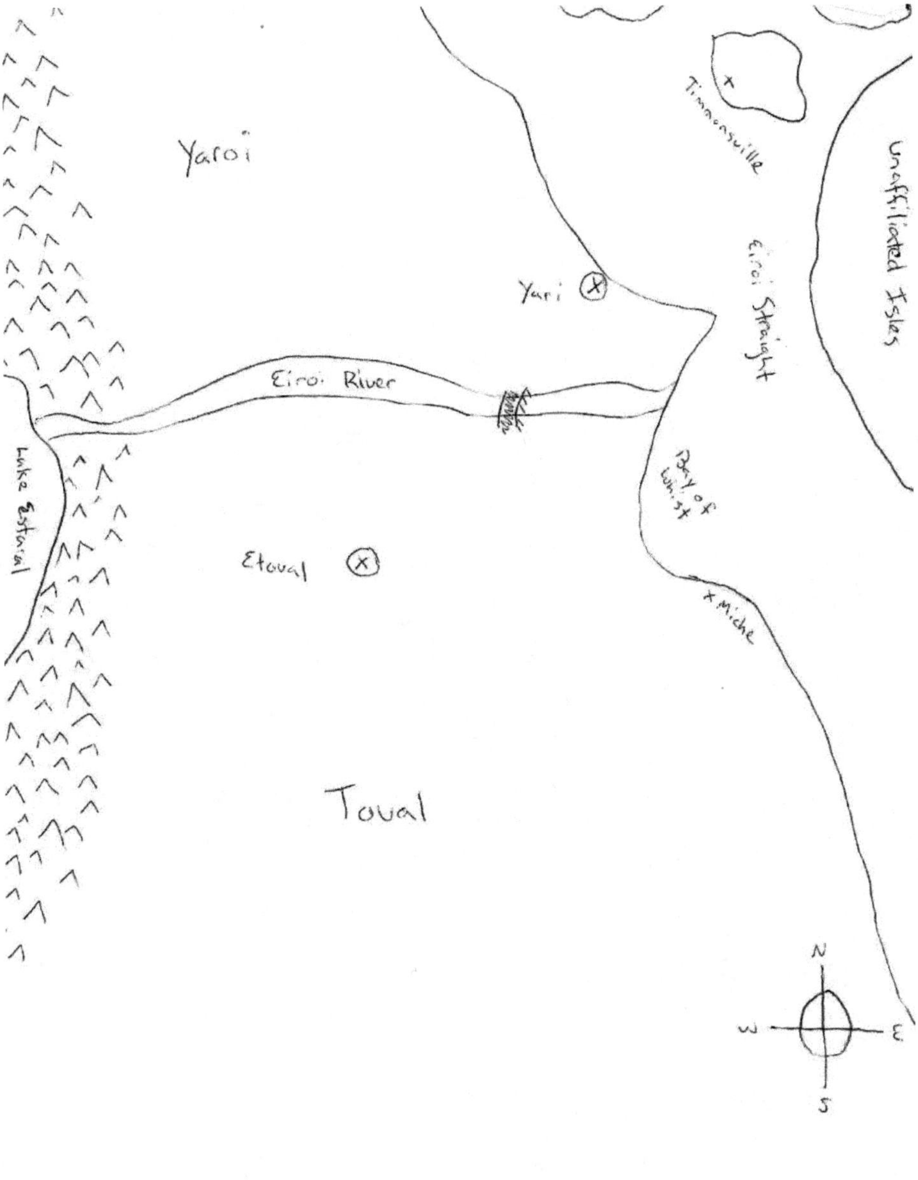

Yaroi
Timmonsville
X
Unaffiliated Isles
Yuri X
Eiroi Straight
Eiroi River
Lake Estoria
Bay of Luhist
Etoval X
X Miche
Toval
N
W E
S

Prologue

AMA KNEW HOW he had gotten into this situation. The Yarokai had excellent noses, so sniffing him out, tracking him down, and capturing him had been far easier than in most of the places Ama went to sneak around. Even his magic hadn't been enough to prevent his capture, warning him too late that he should have taken his chances heading for the border rather than holing up and trying to hide.

What Ama didn't know was how he was going to get out of this with his head still attached to the rest of his body. The Yarokai were, in general, a suspicious bunch, insular, and parochial. Any strangers in the cities within the country of Yaroi received extra scrutiny. Tracking them all had to be difficult, since the majority of Yaroi's cities were coastal trade cities along the Eiroi Strait with merchants, sailors, and travelers from other countries coming and going constantly. They were the main entry port to the rest of the continent for land-based travel too, so Yaroi always had caravans of foreigners crossing through.

Ama had planned to blend in. He arrived at Yaroi's capital city of Yari with a merchant caravan, acting as a guard to deter thieves, and then spent plenty of time each day visibly working to negotiate a contract to leave Yaroi with a different caravan. Only in the quiet hours around noon, when any good Yarokian was meditating and business was never conducted, or in the dark of night, had Ama tried sneaking around.

He had never failed so miserably.

Sensory deprivation was the worst sort of punishment for a Yarokai, so Ama's cell didn't have any windows to allow light or air in. The door was thick wood with only a small flap at the bottom to push meals through. While depriving sight, sound, and smell might be particularly terrible for the Yarokai, it wasn't exactly a walk in the park for Ama either, especially since he was basically convicted before they could put him on stage for a sham trial.

At least Ama would go to his execution knowing his last mission had been successful. Queen Trina would be relieved to know that much. Aunt Millie would be sad to know he was gone, although given her abilities, she probably already knew he was in trouble. She was too far away to help, though, so Ama wasn't counting on that. Aunt Millie knew better too. In her four years since taking the throne in Namin, she had become a good and trustworthy ruler, and Namin was beginning to return to prosperity. She wouldn't do anything to jeopardize that, including engaging with Yaroi on his behalf, particularly after what he had just done. Even if Yaroi didn't use military assets to attack Namin, they controlled the trade from the Eiroi Strait. If they leveled extra tariffs on Namese goods or simply refused to allow Namese goods to be traded through Yaroi ports, Namin's economy would backslide. No, Ama was definitely on his own there.

At least Ama had visited home recently, to see all his aunts, uncles, and cousins, and had visited Namin too. Seeing Aunt Millie was always fun. She had been too busy at the time to really talk though. The last time Ama had actually sat down with her alone for more than a hurried lunch, before she went on to her next meeting and Ama returned to work, had been four years ago, right after her coronation. Ama had hoped her words at the time meant he had a happy future in front of him, but now he knew better. She had meant he shouldn't worry about his future because he would be executed before he had a chance to actually achieve his dreams.

"If you want my advice, I think you should continue adventuring on Prince Braxton's behalf. Have some fun for a few more years, and maybe someday you'll find whatever it is you're actually searching for."

Even Toval, who had assigned him this delicate mission, wouldn't be able to save him. They couldn't admit they had sent him to Yaroi, that they were involved at all, nor that they knew Ama even existed—all for the same reasons Namin wouldn't dare help Ama. No, Ama had to take complete responsibility for this fiasco. That was the only way to save Toval and Namin, as well as to ensure the last parts of this mission were successful.

Ama shifted on the hard stone bench, the only furniture in his cell, and leaned against the rock wall, attempting to get as comfortable as possible. He tried to focus on happier memories as he waited to die.

The first time he had seen Prince Braxton, looking so strong and powerful on a horse as he rode through Ama's home village. Ama making the decision to help Prince Braxton any way he could and going about gathering information so he could convince Braxton to hire him. The second time he had seen Braxton, he had snuck into Braxton's camp and startled him. Once Braxton calmed down, Ama had managed to convince Braxton Ama was only there to share information. That memory made him smile.

Another of his favorite memories was more recent. Namin's aggressions against Toval had grown too much, so Toval had decided to intervene by sending troops to support a coup. Braxton had asked if Ama might be able to find someone suitable to sit on the Namin throne after they removed the king of the time, which meant finding someone capable of wielding Namin's royal magic. Ama had traveled only a few hours before finding Aunt Millie, who had chosen to come to him, to support Ama in Ama's quest to help Braxton in any way the Tovalians needed. Now Aunt Millie was Queen Carmillian of Namin.

Ama couldn't say how much time passed as he sat in the tiny prison cell, inwardly focused on his memories —a couple days, at least, but he couldn't be sure. Food came, but not at regular intervals, so Ama couldn't use that to gauge time. After what felt like a very, very long time, he finally heard the scrape as the lock was turned. The door opened with a slow groan, the light beyond almost blinding Ama. He blinked, trying to clear the spots from his vision, and a grinning guard eventually came into view. A pair of manacles in his hands were held out in Ama's direction.

"Your punishment has been decided," the guard stated as Ama stood and walked over to the door, arms outheld for the guard to place the manacles around Ama's wrists. He didn't say anything more, instead, shoving Ama forward so he stood in the middle of a circle of guards. They walked for a while, the floor sloping slowly upward, only the torches set into the walls at intervals supplying any light. The group paused when they reached a door, then waited for the guard in front to unlock it and pull the door open. He stepped aside and waved for Ama to go through first.

The guards and the excited crowd surrounding the perimeter of the stone-flagged amphitheater just outside the door let Ama get a good look at his punishment for a few long moments. Eager anticipation emanated from the crowd as they let him take it all in. Ama swallowed hard, but his resolve was firm. He would complete his mission no matter what they did to him.

"Anytime you want to tell us everything, this will stop," the guard growled in Ama's ear.

"There's nothing to tell. I didn't do anything wrong," Ama replied. He tried to sound unconcerned, but his throat was dry and stomach clenched. He had hoped for a quick hanging or beheading, not a slow death like this, but either way, he would endure—for the sake of everyone he had to protect.

He had to.

Chapter One

KARL TOOK A deep breath, the fishy, salty smell of the ocean somehow feeling fresh and welcoming. That was probably because he had just spent the last few hours sitting with the rest of the passengers in the hold of the ship he was on, a dank and dark space below deck with stationary hard benches and the stench of too many people in far-too-close quarters. Escaping onto the deck the second the sailors let them know they had arrived was a relief Karl hadn't wanted to pass up. The gangway was still being hooked up, and the customs station beyond didn't have anyone at the table there, so there was still time for Karl to stretch cramped legs from sitting the last five hours.

Beyond the docks appeared a city unlike any other port Karl had ever seen, even for the capital of a country like Yaroi. Warehouses dominated the space around the docks, and narrow roads led to buildings that must be houses and shops. Karl had a fairly good vantage from the height of the ship, but even he couldn't see anything about the town that made it actually as special as the Yarokai liked to crow anytime they had a conversation about it. The only exception was the palace. With delicate spires in glittering white stone and beautifully carved creatures and statues dotting the surface, the palace dominated the northern skyline. This was definitely the jewel of Yaroi, although Karl was well aware of the blackened rot that beauty served to conceal.

"All right, everyone, line up!" one of the sailors called. Karl joined the queue forming at the gangway, slowly moving forward as each person went through customs. At least an hour passed before Karl finally reached the desk. The sun overhead was bright in a nearly cloudless spring sky; Karl shaded his eyes with his hand as he navigated down the gangplank, hoping not to fall into the ocean. Thankfully, the dock itself was covered by the lengthening shadows as the sun dipped lower in the sky. There were still a few hours before sunset, but it definitely was getting late in the day.

"Name?" the woman sitting at the table asked without bothering to look up, focused on the papers she was busy writing on. She held her vowels longer than Karl was used to, even though she spoke the same language as Toval and Namin, but thankfully she was easy enough to understand. Karl had met people from Yaroi whom he couldn't understand at all.

"Karl Musen."

The pen paused and she tilted her head up to glare at him. "You're part of that Musen clan?" she snapped out. She took in a slow breath through her nose, no doubt gauging his scent.

"Adopted, but yes," Karl replied with an easy shrug. He didn't know if she could smell lies or whether she simply wanted his scent for tracking purposes, but he was telling mostly the truth so it didn't matter.

"Where did you embark from?"

"Timmonsville."

She wrote that down. "Purpose in Yaroi?"

"Just passing through."

She kept writing. "Final destination?"

"Miche, in Toval."

She paused in her writing to glare at him again. "Why didn't you take a ship there directly?"

Karl let out a heavy, put-upon sigh. "Because my new employer in Miche didn't provide any funds for me to actually get there, and it's cheaper to hire on with a caravan from Yari than to charter passage through the Eiroi Strait and all the way down to Miche."

Miche was one of the cities along Toval's coast, and it required traversing through the Yaroi-controlled and taxed Eiroi Strait and down the Tovalian-controlled waters of the Bay of Whist. Karl had chosen Miche as his destination on paper because literally the only good thing about Miche was the abundance of fresh fish they pulled out of the bay; the city itself was generally an average place. Miche was also quite a ways southeast of Etoval, the capital city of Toval; any caravan going to Miche wouldn't stop in Etoval since it was so far out of the way. Avoiding anyone thinking Karl was headed to Etoval was very important while he was in Yari.

"Who is your employer?" she asked.

"A bakery there. It doesn't have a name. I was told it's the only bakery on Tickerel Row."

"A Musen going to a bakery?" she asked, and this time her glare was narrow-eyed with suspicion.

"I was adopted," Karl repeated. "The Musen family only paid for me to go to the two-year baking program at Timmonsville, rather than the five-year one for chefs. I graduated last week."

His attending the two-year program at Timmonsville, the premier cooking school, was true enough. As was his being adopted into the Musen family. But Karl had chosen to only go to the baking program rather than obtaining his full chef's license. He knew how to cook well enough—even up to his adoptive father's standards—but Karl's heart would always be with yeast and pies and all things baking related. Not that this customs officer or the rest of Yaroi needed to know any of that.

"How long are you planning to stay in Yari?" she finally asked, her gaze still narrow, but her lips a touch less pinched.

Karl glanced up at where the sun was well past the apex of the horizon. "I suppose it's too late to find a caravan leaving today, so I'll rent a room for the night and see about finding a caravan leaving first thing in the morning." Karl shrugged again. "I can't really afford to stay more than one night."

She snorted and wrote some more on her papers. "Let me see your identity documents, then."

Karl had them ready at the top of his bag, so he passed them over and waited while she read through and compared what was on his documents to what she had written down. Technically, Karl's documentation wasn't a forgery, since the office in Etoval that issued honest paperwork had created his too, but the documents were as truthful as his story. Still, everything matched up. She returned his documents and then signed a slip of paper, which she also handed to him.

"I suggest the Dancing Bell for tonight. Clean, but cheap, and one meal included in the cost." She gave him directions perfunctorily, already looking past him. "Next!"

Karl trotted off, heading deeper into the city. A glance at the slip of paper said she had given him a three-day pass. If he ended up staying in Yaroi longer than three days, he needed to present himself at a custom's headquarters to renew his pass. He needed to show the pass at the city gates when he left as well. Karl carefully tucked it away with the rest of his documents, then followed her directions toward his inn for the night. The city was full of twists and turns, not one road straight, but the directions were accurate. Before long, the spires of the palace towers blocked out the setting sun, so Karl had to start squinting through growing gloom for street signs. Not one lamp was lit outside—Karl didn't even see a lamppost to light in the first place—so it was slow going, but he did eventually find a building bustling with a crowd inside, the picture of a bell hanging from the sign over the front door.

Inside was a narrow entryway just large enough for the small desk and staircase behind it. To the left was a wide opening leading into a tavern completely full with patrons apparently enjoying an early evening drink, although some were also eating. Karl approached an older woman sitting behind the desk.

"The custom's officer said I might be able to rent a room here for the night?" Karl asked.

She nodded. "We have a vacancy, but you have to pay up front if you want dinner tonight."

"Yes, ma'am," Karl replied, already reaching into his tunic for his coin purse. He passed over some coins, and she gave him his change and a key.

"Room six. Dinner is served until nine tonight; if you don't come down, you don't eat, and you forfeit that cost. City curfew is at nine thirty, so be in your room by then, or you'll be bailing yourself out of jail in the morning."

"Thank you, ma'am," Karl replied, nodding to her as he walked around the desk and headed up the stairs. He found eight rooms along a hallway at the top, four doors on each side, and each door had a number burned into the wood. Inside of room six was a perfectly serviceable twin bed and a small table with a washbasin and pitcher on it. Running water hadn't yet made it to Yaroi, at least not to the city of Yari. Timmonsville was in the process of retrofitting the academy, but Karl's home in Etoval had running water. Karl sometimes thought that was what he had missed most over the last two years. For one night, a washbasin would suffice, and hopefully Karl would be home again very soon.

Karl dropped his bag on the bed, slung his coat over the footrail, and headed back downstairs to go find dinner. This was Yaroi, and no one was more suspicious than the Yarokai, so his things would likely be searched while he was eating. Everything in his bags supported his story, though, so Karl wasn't worried. He had clothes, his chef's knives in their travel sachet, sealed closed with a Timmonsville crest, and all his paperwork and correspondence. Literally the only thing in there that could get him in trouble was a rambling letter from his cousin in Miche, expressing at length how excited he was to learn Karl would be traveling to his hometown, and all about how he had gotten Karl the job at the bakery. That one letter was actually in code, one used exclusively by the royal family of Toval for their personal correspondence so it shouldn't be recognized by Yaroi.

Karl settled into an open seat and waved over a barmaid. "I paid for a meal with my room," he told her.

She nodded. "It'll be right up."

She left and Karl let out a heavy breath. No doubt his meal would take a while to arrive to give the searchers plenty of time to go through his bag, but it was still fairly early for dinner so Karl didn't mind waiting too much. Besides, he needed to figure out his next steps.

The Tovalian royal code was simple. An extra curl in the cursive of a letter said how many letters to the left or right to count. Once Karl found all the letters, he could read the actual message.

Operative missing in Yari. Name Ama. Very important to rescue and complete mission. N says find courtyard outside palace dungeon. B

The single N was a reference to Namin, particularly their queen who had the ability to see the past, present, and future, thanks to her royal magic. Every royal family had their own carefully hoarded version of golden-colored royal magic, but Karl thought Namin's was the scariest. Toval's royal family could summon weapons, while Yaroi's had a stronger shapeshifting ability. Karl didn't know what "stronger shifting" actually entailed, just that it was more than the rest of the population. Neither held a candle to what Namin's royals could do.

The B was his Uncle Braxton, chief spymaster for Toval and one of Karl's adoptive father's older brothers. Well, sort of. For political reasons, only one of Karl's fathers was legally his father, Charmaine Musen, who had given Karl his last name. Char was married to Prince Fenwick, Fen, who couldn't officially adopt Karl, but they both raised him anyway.

Karl had his orders, and he was going to do his best to complete them. Tonight he had to find that courtyard and see what had happened to Ama. First, though, he needed to get through dinner.

The barmaid returned, carrying a laden tray. She deposited a bowl of stew, a plate with two crusty rolls, and a mug of beer in front of him. "Enjoy." She smiled at him before leaving. While she seemed friendly enough, the hairs on the back of Karl's neck stood up.

A glance around showed the room was bright enough to conceal any errant flares of light from anyone watching. Karl called on his magic and sent it to explore the food. He didn't have Char's ability to neutralize poison, nor anything fancy like royal magic, but his magic was unique in its own way. Gold-colored magic was exclusive to royal magic. Green was of the body, so healing and military. Blue was household magic, including cooking, cleaning, and construction. Karl's magic was red, which usually had only one purpose: assassination. However, what red magic really held sway over was decay. He could take a perfectly healthy plant and turn it into old fertilizer in seconds, and in some cases, he could reverse the decaying process to bring something back to health—although that was usually to reverse the effects of red magic use. He couldn't heal or bring back the dead.

His magic told Karl the stew was merely simple stew. Beef chunks, carrots, onion, potatoes, and celery. Some beer and spices for flavoring. Karl would have used beef stock, and either okra or dried peas as a thickening agent, but the general taste was acceptable on his palate. The bread was a failure to his baker's eye. The crumb was dense, which either meant their yeast was too old and didn't have the oomph to make the dough rise properly, or they hadn't given it enough time to proof before baking. Possibly both. The crust was flaky with a good crunch and, despite the crumb, did sop up the liquid from the stew, so Karl enjoyed it anyway.

The beer, on the other hand, was drugged. A decent barley beer and a good foam layer at the top that meant the tap wasn't too old, but Karl's magic sensed the extra bit of oddness inside which said something that didn't belong had been added. A sleeping pill, Karl realized, chewing on bread to keep his frown from showing on his face. That was actually convenient.

He flooded the mug with his magic, forcing the contents to age and lose potency. The result was incredibly flat beer with a sharply bitter aftertaste and zero alcohol, but the sleeping drug was neutralized. Karl made sure to drink everything in the mug, killing the terrible taste with bites of stew and bread. When every dish was empty, Karl let out a happy sigh and relaxed into the chair, his legs stretched out in front of him under the table.

Finding the specific courtyard outside the castle dungeon wouldn't be easy. For one, there was no telling how many courtyards surrounded the palace, and Karl didn't know where the dungeons were located. For another, he would need to evade the Yarokai guards. Karl had barely been able to navigate the streets in the hazy light of twilight. The reason the city didn't bother with streetlights was likely because the general population didn't need them; the Yarokai were a step above the general population in ability. Evading the Yarokai was going to be difficult, but, hopefully, not impossible.

As far as Karl was aware, there were four classes of people in Yaroi. The lowest class and the most derided were people without any magic at all. The second lowest class were the people with magic like the rest of the continent, the green, blue, and red magic everyone else in the world used. But not in Yaroi. Yaroikians had their own, unique magic. The highest class in Yaroi were the royals with their golden magic that allowed them some sort of extra abilities with their shapeshifting. However, the most populated class was the middle to upper class, called the Kai. Every single member of the Kai had the ability to shift between human and animal form. Within the Kai were additional subclasses: carnivores above herbivores, and the more dominant and powerful the carnivore, the higher the rank. Nobles were comprised of only the fiercest creatures—wolves, bears, lions, and even snakes—and the rest of the Kai comprised a descending rank of creatures. The lowest rank held creatures like rabbits, but even a rabbit was above a green magic user in societal ranking.

What all that meant was the majority of residents in Yari could see perfectly well in the dark, thanks to their animal abilities, so they didn't bother wasting taxpayer coin on lamps. When Karl snuck out and tried to find this Ama person, he would be at a distinct disadvantage as a mere human with only red magic. However, not only was very little understood about the capabilities of red magic since it was the rarest of the colors, but the Yarokai looked down on it so much Karl doubted they even knew what little was actually publicly available about its uses. Karl could definitely use that to his advantage. First, though, he had to convince anyone watching him that the sleeping drug was definitely going to ensure Karl would be completely incapable of moving again until the morning.

Enough time had probably passed for the drug to begin taking effect. Karl let his head droop so his chin was resting on his chest, and his eyes slid closed. A moment later he started to tilt in his seat, and then jerked upright, blinking blearily around the room. He stood slowly, using the table for leverage, and tottered his way through the crowd and out into the lobby. He knocked into the desk and leaned on it heavily, blinking slowly.

"Sorry," he said to the woman sitting there. "The long day appears to be catching up with me. Do you know what time I should leave here in the morning to get to the caravan staging area in time to book one?"

She smirked at him but quickly covered that with a concerned frown. "Too much travel will do that to a body. Curfew ends at five in the morning, so you should leave here then. I'll have someone come by to wake you just before."

"Is that—" Karl stifled a yawn. "Sorry. Is that going to cost me more?"

"No, no. It's on the house." She lowered her voice to a whisper and leaned closer. "Between you and me, we do it to ensure you're gone from here early. Gives us plenty of time to clean the room for the next occupant, you see."

"Makes sense. Thanks, then. I'll see you in the morning."

Karl gave her a half-hearted wave that showed it was too much work to lift his arm any higher, then toddled to the stairs. He used the banister for leverage as he slowly made his way upward. Only once he was on the upstairs landing, out of sight of any onlookers, did he stand up straight again. He wanted to try out a theory. Smaller inns like this one often didn't bother with the expense of locks with a master key. They were likely to cut corners instead. Karl slid his key into the door with a one burned into it, but nothing happened. He moved down to the door with a two, and the lock clicked open. He quickly relocked it and continued down the hall, going to his own room six and letting himself inside. He locked the door behind him and did a belly flop onto the bed, as if he had lost the strength to lie down like a normal person, hoping the thud was audible downstairs.

The key he had been given for room six apparently opened the even numbered doors, Karl mused as he lay there, his escape plan beginning to form. He rolled over and blew out the candle in the wall-mounted holder over the bed, plunging the room into darkness, and then he didn't move again until after his eyes became accustomed to the darkness. The shade over the window was pulled down, but it was slightly narrower than the window itself, leaving cracks someone outside could peek through if they wanted. As long as he was careful of those angles, he ought to be good for now.

Karl slowly rolled off the bed, landing softly on the floor on the side closer to the door. First he removed his shoes. One, he let topple to the side of the door as if it had been offhandedly tossed there. The other, he planted firmly, sole down into the floor where any attempt at opening the door fully would hit it. The hard sole was slip resistant, designed to be worn in a kitchen where floors could be wet and slippery, and in a contest between the door and the shoe, the shoe would win. The shoe's placement blocking the door only allowed barely enough room for someone to poke their head around the door, or for someone slim to slide through, but anyone of normal size would need to move the shoe to get in and out. This would aid in the illusion that Karl was safely tucked into bed.

Next, he moved into a clear bit of floor, lying on his back so he could do some sit-ups. He rolled over and did some push-ups next, before rolling onto his back again to do more sit-ups. He needed to work up a sweat, but quietly—anything that would get his scent permeating through the room, and all over the clothes he had already been wearing since early this morning without alerting anyone to the sounds of his exercise.

When he was clammy from sweat, Karl stopped. He didn't want to raise his heartbeat too much or start panting for breath or make any noise that might signal he was up to something. He took off his sweaty clothes and used any dry spots on the cloth to wipe any damp areas on his body.

A spare blanket was folded on the floor under the bed. Karl rolled it into a lumpy form approximating the shape of a human curled up into a ball, then placed it under the covers of the bed. On top of the blanket, he draped his stinking clothes.

If anyone tried to peek into the room, the door would get caught on his shoe to prevent them from actually entering quietly. However, they would be able to see what appeared to be a body on the bed from that distance and would smell him clearly.

Now to ensure he wouldn't get caught while out and about. The soap provided with the water pitcher and cloth was distinctly flowery and thereby easily trackable. Karl would use it in the morning to conceal his scent but for now stayed away. He dug into his bag instead, impressed by how well the searchers had returned everything when they were done. The clothes were folded along the correct creases, none of the papers in his folio were bent or wrinkled, and everything was in the same order and organized as before. The only thing Karl saw that indicated the bag had been searched was the slightest melting of the edge of the Timmonsville wax seal over the strings tying his leather knife case closed. The strings were only for show, of course, but they looked legitimate. Karl unhooked one of the strings from a hidden catch and unrolled the case, revealing all of his knives in perfect order. He rerolled the case and set it aside, then returned to digging through his bag. At the very bottom—because the things Karl needed somehow always sank to the very bottom—he found his sliver of travel soap. Tovalian healers had designed the soap to be anti-bacterial, so it would remove all traces of smell from Karl's body, and since it was unscented, he wouldn't add any additional odors he could be tracked with.

Getting clean took only a few minutes, and Karl changed into dark-gray pants and shirt before repacking his bag and setting it back where the searchers had left it. The gray would meld better in the city environment than black, and it looked less suspicious in luggage. Preparations complete, Karl found a space behind the door and out of sight of the window to sit and wait until it was time for the rescue mission to begin.

Chapter Two

THE AMBIENT NOISE from the bar downstairs slowly died down over the next hour or so, but at 9:00 p.m.—when the proprietress said they closed—the noise abruptly stopped completely. Sounds from the street outside Karl's window continued for a bit longer, but by the 9:30 p.m. curfew absolute silence descended over the city, as if it had gone into stasis for the night. Karl remained where he was, leaning against the wall behind him and waiting.

He was dozing lightly, head resting against his bent knees, when the barest scrape and click from the door indicated someone had unlocked it. Karl froze in place, taking slow, shallow breaths so he didn't make any noise. The door bounced off the waiting shoe and a muffled curse followed, and then the shape of a person's head appeared in the narrow opening as a dim outline in the darkened room.

"His damned shoes are in the way," a woman's voice whispered in a low hiss to someone else in the hallway. She sounded like the proprietress Karl had spoken to when he checked in.

"Then he's probably still there," a man's voice whispered back.

"He's lying right there, dead to the world. It stinks of human in here too. I'm gonna need hours tomorrow to scrub out the stench from those blankets." The door clicked shut before the man responded, and muffled footsteps outside the door indicated they'd left.

Karl grinned. His subterfuge had worked. The shoes kept them from actually entering the room, and his smell and the lump in the bed was enough to convince them he was drugged for the night. Now all Karl needed to do was evade anyone watching outside.

Another two hours crept by as he waited, dozing and trying not to make any noise. At approximately midnight, Karl finally stood and stretched, pushing his arms over his head until his shoulders cracked and the accumulated tension in his spine relaxed. By this point, any watching guards would have reached a stage of complacency when their mind was more focused on the nearing end of their shift than on the actual job. Still, Karl needed to be extremely cautious. Yarokians were some of the most suspicious and untrusting people on the continent, so the end-of-shift complacency Karl was used to in Toval might be significantly more relaxed than Yaroi's version.

Karl slowly opened the door to his bedroom and paused, listening at the jamb for any telltale rustle indicating someone had shifted in response. He didn't hear anything, so he opened the door the width his shoe allowed and peeked carefully into the hallway. Still nothing. Karl let out a silent breath of relief before squeezing his body through the narrow opening, glad he was on the smaller side.

If he had to guess, Karl would say the proprietress had gone to bed for the night. The man with her for the earlier searches was likely either downstairs by the front desk where he could listen for any creaks or footsteps, or was outside watching the windows for movement within the rooms belonging to travelers like Karl. Of course, they could also assume after that check-in that the drugs were working and no one was actually watching Karl anymore, but this was Yaroi and it paid to be cautious when any Yarokian was involved.

Karl locked his door and started walking, placing his feet slowly and carefully to avoid the floorboards creaking. Loud snores emanated through the closed door of the room next to Karl's, so he kept moving. The next room along the even side of the hall was the one Karl had tested his key in. He pressed his ear to the wood, listening for any sign someone was inside and awake. Hearing nothing, Karl very carefully slid his key into the lock and turned, only the faintest click audible. Karl pushed the door open only a crack, listening hard, and still didn't hear anything. He let himself inside and quietly closed the door behind him, relocking it before turning to survey the room.

The bed was bare, stripped down to the mattress with no sign of blankets or pillows, and the rest of the room equally empty. Karl let out a relieved breath and moved over to the window. The shade was down, but Karl could still peek outside through where the edges didn't meet the window frame. A glance was all he needed to understand why this room wasn't in use. If the rooms in this inn were primarily to keep track of travelers as they transited through Yaroi, this particular room wasn't situated in such a way to facilitate that. The roof of the entryway below partially blocked the view of the window, and a tree growing in the neighbor's yard had stretched branches between the building, blocking the rest.

Not about to ignore a gift like this one, Karl quickly unhooked the lock on the window and carefully slid it up. He left the shade down, slipping beneath as he climbed outside. Karl only hung from the sill long enough to slide the window down again, before using the entry roof and a convenient tree limb to make his way to the ground where he immediately ducked into the shadows cast by the building in the scant moonlight from the waxing crescent. The air was brisk with the last vestiges of winter, and Karl started walking so the movement could warm him up.

The palace loomed large overhead, a beacon for Karl to follow as he dashed from shadow to shadow, making his way down the streets and closer to whichever palace courtyard Ama was located near. After about forty minutes of slinking around, Karl arrived at what appeared to be an open-air market. All the stalls were shuttered for the night, the space as quiet as the rest of the city. Eerily quiet. In Etoval, the markets never fully shut down for the night. Many stalls did close, but some shifted to accommodate a different sort of clientele. Other shops simply had evening or night clerks, rather than closing. Mage lights kept the areas well-lit, and the guard patrolled regularly. Here, there wasn't even a breeze off the ocean to cut the oppressive silence, the surrounding buildings too tall in the winding streets to allow for even that much relief. Only the pervasive stench from old manure and human sweat indicated the market had ever been alive.

The market might be eerie, but it provided an opportunity Karl wasn't about to pass up. He wandered around from stall to stall, sticking to the shadows in case a guard might be patrolling while still spreading his trackable scent all over the market. His scent might be newer than the previous day's stench, but if the manure and sweat was strong enough for

Karl's human nose to smell, the stronger noses of the Yarokai would be overwhelmed. Finding Karl's scent amid that would be very difficult, especially when the market reopened in the morning and fresh manure and sweat were added to the mix. As Karl meandered, he slowly and carefully called on his magic.

Body sweat was easy to rot, already partially decomposed the moment it touched air. As Karl walked, he focused his magic on his body's sweat. Every step increased the growing putrid stench of a rotten flesh, until his own scent was completely subsumed. Karl swallowed back a gag, breathing shallowly through his mouth as he fought the urge to plug his nose. He wandered through the market for another ten minutes, crisscrossing his previous path to help obfuscate any potential link someone might make between his two scents. Only once Karl felt he had done everything possible, did he return to his goal of finding one courtyard around a massive palace, sliding between shadows as he snuck down the streets ever closer to the looming palace ahead.

Another half hour of walking brought him to the outer wall, built of thick stone blocks with no attempts to coat or seal it. Karl could scale the wall easily if he wanted. For a safety-obsessed city, that was odd and was therefore probably a trap. Karl bared his teeth at the wall, unwilling to get caught in such an obvious ploy, then looked around to see what his other options were. To Karl's right he found a brightly lit area, probably the main gates, he assumed. Better for him to avoid that area too. Instead, Karl went left, sticking to the shadows as he followed the wall, hoping he would find an unmanned gate where he could jimmy the lock.

The last thing Karl expected to find was an abrupt end to the wall. The last stone blocks suddenly stopped, revealing a garden with crushed stone paths and carefully maintained dormant flower beds. The only colors visible were from small evergreen bushes carefully pruned back for winter. This far north, the first bulbs hadn't started peeking out from the earth yet, but back home in Etoval the first green stems would be appearing. He couldn't wait to get home again, but first he had to finish this mission.

Karl remained where he was for a few long moments, crouched in the last bit of darkness cast by the wall and staring out into the open space of the garden for any hint of movement. He saw nothing, not even a decent patch of shadow where someone could be hiding. This had to be another trap, though, same as the wall. Etoval was a very safe city with relatively low crime, yet the royal palace was fully enclosed by a protective wall. It made zero sense that Yaroi wouldn't have the same. Still, this was too good of an opportunity to pass up.

Karl stayed on the very edges of the paths where he wouldn't leave footprints in the soft dirt of the beds, straining his ears for any hint that he had been spotted. He stuck to the perimeter of the garden, where a wall would have stood had there been one, rather than going through the center where he would be more exposed. Moonlight revealed a massive patio on the other side of the garden, attached to what he assumed was the back of the palace. Or the side of the palace. The building was huge and sprawling, as large as it had appeared back in the harbor, so there was no real way to tell what portion of the building Karl was adjacent to. The garden had to be nearly a mile long, as it took him a good twenty minutes to traverse it. The patio was long gone by the time Karl reached the end where the wall appeared again.

The nine-foot-high wall continued along the perimeter of the palace grounds as if it hadn't had a massive hole in it. However, this time he found more than neatly manicured paths. Perpendicular to the big wall was a second, waist-high wall that went from the outer wall all the way to the palace, cutting the palace grounds in half. Every twenty to thirty feet Karl found spaces in the wall that looked like doorways. Karl crept closer, curiosity winning over caution, but tensed on the balls of his feet to run just in case. At the first of the doorways, he crouched by the wall, trying to stay in the shadows, and peeked around the wall to take a look. Karl swallowed back a horrified gasp when he saw what was on the other side.

Each doorway led to a downward staircase allowing entry into a small amphitheater. Aside from the stairs, all the rest of the perimeter space was comprised of stone benches for seating. A flat space filled the bottom. The entire amphitheater was approximately a third of the size of the coliseums throughout Namin, spaces Queen Carmillian was slowly turning into theaters and playhouses, rather than fighting rings full of blood and death. The Yarokian version was a thousand times worse. At the bottom, where everyone spectating could see, a table stood with chains for wrists and ankles at the head and foot, and a wheel attached to those chains to stretch the body in cruel torture. This was a terrible torture chamber with seats for over a hundred people to spectate.

Karl swallowed back his disgust and moved to the next amphitheater. The best victims of torture were prisoners, so he had to be near the dungeon and the courtyard where Queen Carmillian said Ama was being kept. The second amphitheater was completely empty, not even a torture apparatus at the bottom. The third had a cold firepit with a rack full of metal implements, and the fourth, another long table with chains, except this time without the wheel. He had no idea what it was used for, but he really, really didn't want to know either. Swallowing bile, this time from everything he had seen rather than his own pervasive stench, Karl moved on to the fifth, and thankfully last, amphitheater. This time, he found a whipping cross only, unlike the others, it was occupied by a body hanging from ropes.

A glance at what was left of the poor man left hanging there was all Karl needed to learn why the scent-based Yarokian trackers hadn't noticed him sneaking onto the palace grounds. It turned out, masking his own scent with rot had been an excellent idea, because the absolute, putrid stench of rotting death emanating from inside that amphitheater was a thousand times worse than anything Karl's magic could ever conjure up. If he hadn't already been partially nose-blind thanks to his own smell, Karl definitely would have thrown up. As it was, he had to plug his nose and breathe shallowly through his mouth to prevent that. Even breathing was vile, the air viscus and heavy as if the stench gave off a physical miasma.

Karl had to continue on with his search. He could only hope a fresh breeze would blow when he returned to the garden. Yet at the same time, he dreaded what he might find next. He looked around for some way to go around the amphitheaters and continue his way around the garden, or better yet, into the dungeons where this Ama was likely being held. He squinted through the gloom and shadows, trying to see around the bottom of the amphitheater, searching for a doorway. This amphitheater was closest to the palace wall, so if there was a doorway, it was most likely to be in this one. Karl couldn't be sure, but he thought he might see an outline to the right of where the body hung. Which meant, unfortunately, he had to go down there where the smell was likely to be unbearable. Still, seeing the dead body left to hang there was all the evidence Karl needed to convince him that saving Ama from a similar repugnant fate was essential.

Karl had worked with the Tovalian military for a little over two years.

Before that he was a street urchin and thief. Death wasn't a stranger for him, nor was seeing dead bodies. Yet, he still hesitated at the top of the stairs, trying not to shudder at the idea of getting closer to that hanging form. Whatever the Yarokai had done to the poor person to leave his corpse in such a disgusting state wasn't something Karl really wanted to see up close. He finally steeled his nerve and placed his foot on the top step to head down when the body's head suddenly turned to rest the opposite cheek against the wooden cross. The rotting corpse was somehow still alive! Karl's feet dashed down the stairs before his brain fully engaged. He slid his belt knife free to cut the ropes holding the body to the cross when he reached the bottom but paused in shock as he took in what was left of the body's back.

The flesh looked melted where it wasn't grossly swollen and leaking some sort of dark-colored pus in even lines across the body, from shoulders down to upper thighs. Karl unfortunately knew of two ways to achieve the melted result he was looking at, poison being the easiest. The problem with that assessment was any poison strong enough to literally melt flesh would have spread outward from those original lines and started melting the entire body, too, and Karl didn't see any evidence of that here. That meant the other method Karl knew of to create this result had to have been used instead—assassin's magic.

One of the first magic lessons Karl had ever learned when he was still a street kid was that pain caused by red magic could only be soothed by red magic. No other healing could fix the damage unique to assassin's magic. Admittedly, the majority of the time the victim of red magic was dead, so using power to fix it was irrelevant at that point. This victim, however, was still breathing, his chest rising and falling very, very slowly, hitching as if each movement hurt—which it probably did. Which meant in this case, Karl could do something to help.

The man's dark eyes were open and looking at Karl when Karl approached, shining feverishly as they reflected the moonlight.

"I didn't tell. They're safe. I didn't tell." The voice was reedy and cracked, a mere whisper as if it was taking all the strength he could muster just to get those words out.

"Let me help," Karl whispered back.

His hand glowed red as Karl called on his magic. He showed the glow to the man, whose eyes widened in surprise. Karl moved to the man's back, holding his hand over the mess of melted flesh, pus, exposed bone and muscle, and swollen pustules. Karl didn't touch, unwilling to cause the man any additional pain, instead, directing his magic in a steady flow from a few centimeters above the mess.

The wounds didn't want to heal, resisting his magic as the red flowed over the man's back. Whoever had caused this hurt originally had really strong powers and was definitely highly trained in using it to hurt. Karl was also highly trained, but not with the same terrible intention. He gritted his teeth and bore down, forcing his magic to overcome all resistance. Slowly, ever so slowly, the worst of the pus started to shrink and some of the exposed bone began to vanish beneath renewed muscle and skin.

"Hide." The voice was a little stronger, but still a faint whisper. Karl lessened his focus on his magic to listen, then heard what the man must have—a tuneless whistle slowly coming closer. "A guard's coming on their rounds," the man added.

Chapter Three

KARL LET HIS magic fade, the glow immediately disappearing, and cast around frantically for somewhere to go. The space was empty aside from the cross and lone occupant; no furniture or structures for Karl to hide behind. The doorway he had seen from above was flush with the wall. The only option Karl could see was a patch of shadow to the left of the steps, cast by the angle of the setting moon. Karl scrambled there, ducking down and tucking his chin into his collar so his face and any exposed skin was concealed behind his dark clothes. He tried to breathe shallowly, attempting to prevent any movement from giving him away or from them seeing his breath misting in the cool night air, and hoped whoever was approaching didn't come down into the amphitheater. In the dark and from high above, Karl thought he might be able to stay hidden, but the same wouldn't be true from the floor where Karl was.

"Hey, stinky, you still alive?" The voice came from above, from what sounded like the top of the stairs, and was dripping with scorn and derision. "Stiiiinnnkkkeeee." The catcall was like nails on a chalkboard, piercing and shrill and completely lacking in any trace of alarm that would indicate the speaker could see Karl.

Karl peeked at the man on the cross, who let his head flop against the wood as if he had tried and failed to look up at the speaker. Karl could have hugged him. Hopefully that would be enough to convince the guard to stay up there.

"Well, damn. Not dead yet. Never fear, stinky, I'll be back to check on you again soon!" The tuneless whistling resumed, fading slowly as the guard continued onward.

Karl waited, trying to stem the rising sense of relief, listening hard for the guard until he was straining his ears to hear the whistle. Only once he was certain the guard was gone, did he scramble back to his feet. Magic sprang to his hands as he returned to his efforts on the man. Flesh continued to reappear in the places it had melted until the white of bone was completely gone and skin regrew over muscle. The puss and pustules shrank until they vanished, taking the worst of the stench with them. Karl kept his magic flowing, searching until he was certain no trace of red magic remained anywhere in the man's body.

A terrible mess still remained, even lines from upper thighs to neck slowly oozing blood from where scabs hadn't yet been able to form. Karl had no ability to heal whip lashes, so unfortunately there wasn't anything he could do to help with that, but at least he could finally cut the man down.

"Who are you?" the man asked as Karl pulled his belt knife free again and started sawing at the thick rope securing one of the man's arms to the cross.

"Hopefully, a friend," Karl replied. He paused in his sawing to hold out the back of his right hand, concentrating to focus his magic until the seal embedded there activated. On most people, the pattern of the House of Etoval glowed green for military magic, but Karl's red magic always over-powered it so the seal was an eerie red-brown in the darkness. Still, it denoted who Karl was working for better than his saying it aloud.

Karl resumed sawing at the rope, finally freeing one arm. He started to walk around to the other side when the man waved his freed hand.

"Definitely a friend," the man said, and a moment later a green seal in the same pattern of the House of Etoval appeared. The green had an odd tone to it, likely for a similar reason to why Karl's was a brownish-red, but Karl was too happy to see the seal to want to overthink it for the moment. "My name is Ama. Who are you?"

"Karl," Karl replied, letting out a relieved breath at the knowledge he was busy rescuing the correct person. He didn't know what he would have done if this man hadn't been Ama. "I was sent to find you by some mutual friends," he added as he started to work at freeing the other arm.

"Those mutual friends should have let me die. Yaroi is going to retaliate when they find out I'm gone, and it won't be pretty."

Karl grunted as the rope around the left hand finally cut through. "I'm going to free your feet now, so hold on to something." He ducked down and carefully slid the knife between Ama's ankles and the rope, then started sawing. "The two people who organized my being here are both aware of the consequences, and I'm sure are already preparing to respond. Besides, Yaroi might suspect they're involved with whatever you were doing here or with your rescue, but unless they catch one of us, they won't have any proof. So let's get out of here before the guard comes back."

The last rope finally broke and Ama let out a little whimper as his arms and abused back muscles suddenly had to take all of his weight. Karl jumped up and carefully gripped Ama under the arms, helping to lower him to the ground.

"Can you walk?" Karl asked, still holding on to Ama.

"Walk, yes," Ama replied, breathing heavily between gritted teeth. "Bleeding everywhere and leaving a trail for them to follow is more of an issue right now."

"You can wear my shirt," Karl replied, already starting to shrug out of the sleeves, for the first time registering that Ama wasn't wearing any clothes. "The cloth should absorb the blood. I can get you more clothes and bandages at my hotel room." He yanked the shirt over his head and handed it to Ama, who hissed in pain as he slowly pulled it on.

"Let's go," Ama said, leading the way to the stairs. At the top he paused, looking both ways for a long moment before moving as quickly as possible in the direction of the outer wall.

Karl stayed tight on Ama's heels, following closely as they reached the spot where the wall tapered into the garden, open to the neighborhood next door.

"I don't understand this configuration," Karl muttered even as he looked around to see if there was any movement.

"It's an illusion. The houses on the other side of the road are actually part of the guard complex. I'm shocked we haven't seen any guards yet, to be honest. People shouldn't be able to simply waltz past the edge of the wall without being spotted like this."

Karl had an answer to that mystery, at least. "They're probably hiding from the smell. I don't know if you could smell what they did to you, but it really wasn't pleasant. In fact, that's an understatement. And I'm using my magic right now to keep that stench going to mask our scent trail."

"Then let's take advantage of it before they realize their lapse." Ama walked around the wall and onto the road, then started walking quickly along the road parallel to the wall until they reached a cross street. Ama went left, away from the looming palace. Every once in a while, Ama's steps would hitch and he'd suck in a breath, so Karl tried to stay close in case Ama needed a hand.

They continued at their current awkward pace for a few long minutes, Karl glancing up at the darkened windows as they passed, hoping none of the watchers enforcing the curfew were nearby since he and Ama didn't bother hiding in the shadows.

"Which hotel did they put you in?" Ama asked as he slowed, his voice soft so he didn't wake anyone sleeping in the houses nearby.

"The Dancing Bell. Which is…" Karl glanced around and realized he was completely lost. "Somewhere. I actually need to get to a market near the hotel, where I can stop the rot stench."

"I think I know the one you're talking about," Ama replied. "Come on."

He resumed his fast pace, and Karl followed. Ama randomly cut down alleyways and wove his way through the streets. While nothing looked familiar to Karl, the palace was farther away every time he glanced in that direction. Suddenly, Ama stopped at the end of yet another alleyway. He looked around as Karl joined him, and Karl realized they had reached the exact market Karl had walked around about two hours earlier.

"This is it," Karl said, grinning at Ama. "Now I just need to dissipate the rot stench while using it to cover up our real scents, and then we can head to my hotel room for the rest of the night."

Before Ama could respond, an eerie howl rang out, echoing between the buildings and sending a shiver down Karl's spine.

"They've realized I'm gone," Ama said instead of whatever he had been about to say a moment earlier, glancing around with a frown. "Look, are you planning to take a caravan out in the morning?" He waited only long enough for Karl to nod before continuing. "Good. There's one going into Toval—the one I was supposed to leave with if I hadn't been caught. They'll still be waiting for me. In the morning, find that caravan. I suspect it's led by someone you'll find familiar, so locating it shouldn't be too hard. Pretend you don't know him, but make sure to contract with that caravan. I promise I'll find you outside the city tomorrow if you're with them. Now, get back to your hotel room. The streets will be crawling with guards in a few minutes." He nodded once, before turning and heading off, back into the depths of the city before Karl could voice any sort of protest.

Karl stared after Ama for a long moment, wishing he dared rush after Ama to bring him back, but a second eerie howl rang out, reminding Karl that time was limited. He didn't have time to argue with Ama, and Ama had seemed confident they would be able to meet up again. All Karl could do at this point was trust him.

Instead, Karl wandered around the market a second time, letting the rotting scent fade as quickly as he dared as he shut off his magic. He made sure to go over the spot where Ama left when the rot was still strong and cancelled the magic completely only once he was on the opposite side of the market. A third eerie howl rang out as Karl finally left the market, the sound dogging his heels as he retraced his steps back to the hotel.

Thankfully, he didn't see or hear any sign of the searchers being nearby. He arrived at the hotel faster than he probably should have, throwing caution away in return for expediency, but it paid off when he reached the tree beneath the window he had left unlocked. Climbing the tree, pushing open the window, and slithering into the empty room took mere seconds. Once the window was firmly closed and locked behind him, Karl could finally afford to breathe.

Yes, his scent was all over that market, but the rot would do a lot to mask it. Couple that with the fact that his scent was in no way associated with Ama's, and that he had a solid alibi of being drugged and asleep, and Karl felt he had a fairly good chance at getting away with tonight's activities. Only time would tell, but first he needed to be back in his room to ensure his alibi held up.

Karl headed to the doorway, listening at the jamb for a good minute for any sign someone was waiting, before unlocking the door and heading into the, thankfully, unoccupied hall. He relocked the door to number two and placed his feet carefully as he then crept to his own room. Karl remembered the shoe being in the way a millisecond before he bounced the door off it; instead, opening the door just enough so he could slip through the narrow opening. Locking the door behind him was the best feeling, almost better than realizing he had actually found Ama.

Karl stripped off his pants and dumped them on his bag, then went to the bed where he dug out his stinking clothes and added them to the pile. He unrolled the used extra comforter and draped it over the edge of the bed as if he had kicked it off in his sleep. Chores done, Karl crawled onto the mattress, curling up under the sheet and blanket.

He wanted to unpack everything that had just happened, and he knew worries over whether Ama had escaped their pursuers would be swirling through his head. Sleep would no doubt be hard coming. Karl closed his eyes, ready for a restless few hours, but was asleep moments later.

Chapter Four

BANG. BANG. "SIR, this is your morning wake up! Curfew ends in fifteen minutes!" *Bang. Bang.* "Good morning, sir!"

Karl groaned as he rolled over, and then a jolt of adrenaline flashed through him when he had to forcibly stop himself from rolling off the bed. He had gotten maybe two hours of sleep, and he felt like it.

Bang. Bang. "Sir, this is your morning wake up!" the woman called through the door a second time, repeating what sounded like her normal morning mantra. "Curfew ends in fifteen minutes!" *Bang. Bang.* "Good morning, sir!"

Karl coughed to clear his throat and replied, "I'm awake! Thanks!" The banging on his door stopped and a moment later more banging started farther away as she moved on to another door.

Getting out of bed basically required completing the epic flop to the floor he had stopped just a moment ago. He bumped his elbow on the edge of the bed and the thud was more dramatic than he intended, but quite frankly, he felt like he had actually been drugged. A long day of travel coupled with the night's adventure and copious overuse of his magic was apparently too much to handle with only two hours' sleep.

Karl dressed and stuffed his things into his bag, then went over to the washbasin to clean his face. He finally moved his shoes from the doorway, sitting on the edge of the bed to pull them on. A quick check around the room and he didn't find anything he had left behind. Walking out into the hallway like a normal person with no need to be cautious was a nice change. Unlike last night, Karl didn't have to feign exhaustion as he reached the foot of the stairs and the front desk.

"Hard night?" the young man sitting there asked.

Karl grimaced. "I slept like a log, and I still feel like I need a few hours more. The travel yesterday must have exhausted me more than I thought." He shrugged. "Hopefully, I can hire on to a caravan that will have space for me to sit or today is going to be difficult."

The young man laughed. "Let me get you some tea. On the house." He went into the tavern area and returned a moment later with a steaming teacup. "You have about five minutes until curfew ends," he added as he passed the cup over for Karl to take. "I can't let you leave until then."

Karl blew on the tea to cool it. He also sent a tendril of magic in to see if anything had been added and found some sort of caffeine additive was dissolved in there. While the caffeine was certainly welcome when he was this tired, it was calibrated to help him dissipate the last of the drugs. He zapped it with magic to decay some of the caffeine, weakening it, and then took a slow sip.

"It's fine," Karl replied. "I'm still waking up. Thanks for the tea." He blew on the tea some more and took another sip. "Can you tell me the best way to get to where the caravans are staged to head to Toval? I'm traveling to the coast."

The man grinned and nodded, going to the window next to the doorway. "Palace is right there, yeah?" He pointed to the looming building starting to reflect the edge of dawn sun peeking over the horizon. "Keep it to your right when you're walking, and you can't miss it. About a five-minute walk from here."

"Thanks." Karl finished his cup and was in the act of handing it back to the receptionist when bells began tolling.

"And curfew has ended for the day. Thanks for staying with us!" The receptionist grinned as he slipped past Karl to flip the lock on the front door.

"The bed was comfortable," Karl replied with an answering smile. "I don't know if I'll ever get the chance to come back this way, but if I do, I'll definitely stay here again."

He walked into the street. The rising sun provided just enough morning light for the road to be visible, which was a nice change. Karl started walking, keeping the directions in mind as he went. He had to retrace part of his path from the previous night, walking toward the palace, but at the first cross street he turned left to ensure the palace was to his right side, then kept going.

Almost exactly five minutes later, Karl walked into some sort of massive parade grounds. Even rows of wagons, horses, or oxen picketed nearby filled the entire space. Thankfully, a sign at the entrance said to continue straight for Toval, so he had some idea of where to go in the morass he waded into. The noise was incredible, escalating louder and louder the farther Karl walked. People were shouting to be heard, buying and selling from the caravans and trying to attract attention of passersby. Animals brayed, children screamed as they played, and everything that could be making noise made as much noise as possible. Some of the caravans had erected tents and put out tables to sell and hung decorations that chimed and clacked in the breeze.

Karl didn't stop to admire the organized chaos, or even to shop, which his sister Emily would razz him for when he told her. Somewhere in this mess was the caravan Ama had told him to find. Every few rows another sign pointed him onward, until he finally reached one that pointed to the right for Toval.

He slowed down as he walked, carefully studying each person he saw. Ama said Karl would recognize the caravan leader, but each group he passed were only strangers.

"Are you looking for a caravan to join to head to Toval, sir?"

Karl turned to look at the girl who had spoken and nearly yelped when he saw Emily standing there. She had tied her brown hair back in pigtail-style braids and wore the dress of a young girl, perfect for her age of ten. Her eyes were the exact same shade of golden brown as Karl's, but that was the only feature they had in common from their shared father. Karl assumed they both looked like their mothers, who were different. Emily still needed to grow into her features, so it was hard to say exactly how they compared. Karl was tall at five foot eleven, and he knew his shoulders and arms were well-muscled from all the kneading he did, but otherwise he thought he was well-proportioned. His hair was brown, too, but a darker shade than Emily's. His nose was a touch wide for his face, but above his full lips, he didn't think that was too noticeable. Whereas, Emily had a cute little button of a nose and the fierce air she had learned from her adoptive mother that said what she looked like was irrelevant because she was powerful no matter what.

The biggest difference between them was their magic. Karl had red magic, but Emily had green healing magic. She hated it, because healing didn't help make her a better fighter—or at least that was what she thought. Karl dreaded the moment she realized the uses being a healer could add to her fighting prowess. What it meant was that if Ama had reached them last night as Karl hoped, Emily would have healed the wounds Karl's magic wasn't able to touch.

However, Emily was supposed to be safely in Etoval under the protective wing of her adoptive mother, Captain Patricia Zain of the Royal Guard, who was teaching Emily weapons and military leadership, much to Emily's delight. That was one of the many reasons Zain had adopted Emily, while Char had taken in Karl and their third sibling Shan. Shan wasn't blood related to Karl and Emily, but he was their brother all the same, a brother of the heart.

Karl wanted to ask Emily so many questions, to demand answers, but he knew better. Instead he gritted his teeth, forced a smile, and managed to nod cordially.

"I am. Is your caravan going to Toval?"

"We are!" She grinned happily at him, fully into her act of eager caravan child. The normal Emily was much more stoic and practical, rather than this obnoxiously bubbly scrap with the adorable grin and wide eyes.

"Are you going to the coast, or inland?" Karl asked. He looked over at the caravan they were in front of and found Ralph leaning against the table where their wares were laid out, his eyes sparking with mirth even as he hid his grin behind a stern frown.

Ralph was Fen's third in command, promoted after Jensen took Captain Wong's spot when he retired a few months back. Karl was most used to seeing him acting as Char's bodyguard, since Ralph was easily the best swordsman in Etoval, and, in fact, likely all of Toval too. Fen, or Commander Prince Fenwick of the Royal Forces, was fourth in line to the throne, but in all the years Karl had known him, Fen was more of an adoptive father to Karl than his commanding officer. Fen might not have been able to officially adopt Karl or Shan, but he was as much of a parent to them as Char. Jensen had acted more in the commander role, especially since Karl had been sent to the Royal Forces to work off his conviction for attempted pickpocketing and was placed under Jensen's watch.

Karl had then snuck Shan and Emily into the military complex, which led to all sorts of shenanigans. Four years later, here they were.

"The coast," Ralph replied as Karl followed Emily closer. "We go through every city from Yari all the way down the entire coast of Toval. You looking to head to one of those, kid?"

"Miche. How much do you charge?"

"Depends on whether you're willing to be an active participant as part of the caravan, or whether you're cargo instead."

"I'm happy to pitch in. I just finished school at Timmonsville for baking, but I'm a fair hand at cooking."

"You help with that all the way to Miche, and I might pay you!" Ralph joked. "You in?"

Karl nodded. "Yes. When do you leave?"

"Just getting in a few more sales during the after-curfew rush. And to let the crowds at the gates die down a bit. Maybe by seven, we'll head out. That good for you?"

"Since I don't have anywhere else to stay tonight, leaving today is perfect."

"Great! Come on back, and I'll introduce you to everyone."

Ralph clapped Karl on the shoulder when he got close, squeezing his fingers comfortingly. Emily skipped past, scrambling up into the main wagon. She made a racket even over the already insane amount of noise around them. Ralph took the opportunity to lean in close and whisper "We've got him. We were just waiting for you. We'll get packed up and get moving right away."

Karl sucked in a breath, relief making his knees weaken, but he managed to climb up after Emily and grab her in a hug after Ralph closed the doors behind them.

"Who did you kill to get sent here?" he asked, squeezing until she squirmed.

"No one important. It was better for me to be out of Etoval for a few weeks, so they sent me here," she added.

"Why? What happened?" Karl asked, holding her out at arm's length and giving his patented older brother glare.

She shrugged. "Some important people wanted me for a meeting of some kind. I told them I was at drill. Mama Zain said some bad words to them, and they went to complain at Uncle Fen. Then Uncle Braxton came by and suggested I come out here."

And since the matter didn't include swords, military strategy, or some new fighting technique, Emily hadn't learned anything more. Karl knew that without even having to ask her for any sort of clarification or actual details. He would have to ask Ralph, but later. Once they were out of Yari, or he might have to wait until they had crossed the Eiroi River into Toval—depending on how sensitive the information. Either way, Karl would get someone to tell him what was going on.

"Hey, if you're done stowing your belongings, we could use some extra pairs of hands out here!" Ralph called, banging on the side of the caravan.

Emily slid out from Karl's grip. She took in a slow breath, and as she released it her façade of perky, overly happy child slid into place.

"Coming!" she chirped out and vanished out the door.

Karl looked around the inside of the caravan to find a spot to stow his bag where it wouldn't slide during transport. The caravan itself was completely enclosed, the insides stocked floor to ceiling with shelves, leaving only the narrow aisle in the middle to walk. Karl found a spot between two small barrels near the front to tuck his bag between, before following Emily back outside into the din, hoping they would be able to get out of Yari and completely out of Yaroi quickly so he could finally get home again.

Chapter Five

THE LAND GATES to leave Yari were impressive: massive stone edifices set in the wall encircling the city with huge wooden doors in the portion open to the countryside beyond. Karl finished munching on filled sweet rolls, which he had bought for breakfast from a vendor along their way, as the four horses pulling the caravan came to a stop in the line of people and wagons waiting to leave.

"Line's a little long today," Ralph remarked, frowning and looking up at the angle of the rising sun. "I hope it moves quickly, or we won't reach our campsite before dark."

"They're searching everyone," the woman standing at the back of the caravan in front of them in line said, scowling. "Sounds like a prisoner escaped."

"That's terrible!" Ralph gasped, as if completely and genuinely shocked. "Hopefully they find them quickly!"

They inched their way forward over the next hour, the line moving incredibly slow and Karl's anxiety rising with every moment. His personal scent was in that market; if one of the people at the gate had somehow smelled him there amid all the other scents, including the rancid one he had created, he wasn't going to get out of Yari. Plus, per Ralph, Ama was hidden somewhere safe in the caravan. Karl couldn't see any secret hinges or places where there was extra space to hide a grown man, but he didn't have the sight or smell of the Yarokai.

They finally reached the front of the line, where guardsmen in chainmail and what appeared to be large dogs in chainmail shirts were searching everything. Those weren't dogs though. They were wolves, the shapeshifted form of the Yarokai. Wolves had the best noses. One of the guards snapped out "Papers" even as two wolves started sniffing everyone. A third wolf circled the wagon, sticking his nose into every nook and cranny.

The horses let out unhappy whinnies when the wolves came too close, a sound Karl wished he could also make when one of the guards stopped in front of him. Karl held out the slip of paper he had been given, stating when he had arrived and when he was supposed to leave. The guard yanked it out of Karl's hands, reading it quickly but thoroughly, before thrusting it back at Karl and moving on to Emily.

"Open it," another guard snapped at Ralph, pointing to the caravan door which was locked closed for travel.

Ralph obeyed, climbing up and quickly unlocking the padlock and unhooking the thick straps holding the door closed. Inside, all of the caravan's wares were carefully stowed away in labeled wooden boxes affixed to the floor or walls so they wouldn't slide. The table they used to display their wares was also strapped down, leaving barely enough space for the gray wolf who jumped inside to thoroughly sniff everything.

When the wolf jumped down, inspection completed, and then stood for a moment next to Ralph as Ralph began the process to close and lock the door, Karl realized just how large those wolves were. On four legs, the top of the wolf's back came up to Ralph's hip, and he was easily as long as Ralph was tall. Powerfully muscled, with sharp teeth revealed as the wolf panted, and claws at the end of each paw, Karl had little doubt the wolf could kill him just as easily as the human-shaped guard with his sword.

Karl waited, trying to appear bored and unconcerned even as every snapped command by one of the guards or snuffle by one of the wolves had him suppressing a nervous jump. Finally, all three wolves and all the human guards gathered off to the side. The lead guard was still scowling, but he waved to say they could move onward.

Karl firmly tamped down on any feelings of relief. He couldn't afford to relax now, not when this was likely the moment of the most scrutiny. After just surviving such a thorough search, now was the moment most people would let their guard down and accidentally reveal something they shouldn't. If Karl was one of the Yarokai, this was the time he would be watching the caravans closest.

Tilly scrambled to grip the lead horse's bridle, guiding him forward. The horses were all too glad to move past the wolves and stepped readily forward but then let out a disgusted snort when they came to a stop only twenty yards farther. They had reached the actual gates, but a woman sitting behind a table and the two guards standing at her back provided their next obstacle before they could leave the city.

"Bring your papers forward," one of the guards called out, sounding like he was tired of repeating the same line over and over.

The group obeyed, Tilly waiting with the horses until Marc was done at the front of the line and could take her place. Karl was in the middle, so he was able to watch as the woman looked over each paper and stamped it before moving on to the next person. Karl handed her his paper when he reached the front of the line.

"How much are they charging you for this trip?" she asked, glancing over at the caravan before looking at him again.

"We bartered," Karl answered truthfully. "Since I graduated from Timmonsville, they're happy for me to cook and keep camp in exchange for being allowed to travel with them."

"Sounds like a good deal," she replied absentmindedly as she stamped his form, already looking past Karl to the next person.

Karl moved out of Emily's way, standing near Ralph in plain sight of the guards. The stamp was in red ink, a blurred circle that was probably supposed to be an animal of some kind, with two equally blurred animal figures in the center.

"They're magical creatures," Tilly explained when she saw him studying the stamp. "Outside circle is a dragon. That's supposed to be a gryphon, and the other blob is allegedly a phoenix. It's the crest of Yaroi." She pointed up at the flag flying on top of the gate. Despite flapping in the wind, the dragon, gryphon, and phoenix were easy to make out.

Karl looked back at the red blobs on his paper and muttered, "they need better stamps."

Tilly laughed and thumped him on the back. "It gets the job done. Now, come on. You don't want to be the reason we're delayed getting out of here. We're going to need to move fast to get to our first campsite tonight since we're running a bit behind."

Only a few minutes later everyone had their papers stamped and one of the guards waved them along. Karl fought to keep his face blank, so the relieved smile threatening to stretch his lips wasn't visible as he walked through the tunnel underneath the curtain wall and out into the sunshine on the other side. They were out of Yari—barely—but they still had the entire length of Yaroi to traverse before they reached the Eiroi River and crossed into Toval. He focused on the hours of walking ahead, and on how much he knew his feet were going to hurt, and that dangerous smile faded away.

"Let's move!" Ralph called, setting the pace to a brisk walk that ate up the ground but didn't tax the horses pulling the wagon.

The caravan ahead of theirs was two wagons pulled by oxen moving considerably slower. They reached the caravan and went around it, the road, thankfully, more than wide enough, and the woman they had spoken with while they waited in line waved as they went past.

Karl had remained in good shape while at Timmonsville. He had run a couple miles every day and done the fighting exercises before bed every night, plus he had completed the marathon sessions of kneading and baking for the school that were honestly more strenuous than anything the Royal Forces had ever had him do. Despite all that, he was panting by the end of the first mile of fast walking. After the second mile Karl started eying the seated space at the very front of the wagon where Tilly was serenely holding the reins and guiding the horses behind Ralph's lead. Emily was happily skipping along on the other side of the wagon, not winded in the least. Marc followed along behind to watch their rear, and he also didn't appear bothered by the pace.

They weren't running, and their pace wasn't anything out of the ordinary—Ralph would never be that careless—so there was no reason for Karl to be puffing along so heavily. And yet, the long day of travel and the fraught, sleepless night were taking their toll. He felt exhausted all the way down to his bones.

They caught up with another caravan sometime during the third mile and had to slow. This caravan was six wagons and had multiple kids running around; it took a while to coral them all and move to the side to give enough space for Ralph and their single wagon to slip by.

Karl went up to the front of the wagon where Tilly sat and called up to her. "Can I join you?"

"Feeling your age today?" she asked, already sliding over to give him space. Karl gratefully found handholds and climbed up.

"More like last night took more out of me than I realized," he muttered to her in an undertone. "Give me a few minutes to catch my breath, and I'll get out of your way."

"Take as much time as you like," she replied, laughing.

Karl took her at her word. He braced his feet on the running board as they finally got around the kids and their massive caravan and picked up speed again. He meant to only stay up there until he had his wind back and his legs were less shaky. Instead, he managed about five whole minutes before he fell asleep.

Chapter Six

SOMEONE WAS POKING his shoulder. Karl groaned and batted at the pestering finger and tried to curl into a tighter ball.

"It's lunch. You have to get up if you want food."

Emily's voice penetrated through, and consciousness slowly began to filter in. He wasn't in the room he shared with Shan at the Royal Forces barracks. Nor was he in the narrow bed in the closet-sized room he had been allotted at Timmonsville. His back ached differently right now than that terrible mattress had ever caused. Karl slowly opened his eyes, blinking at the narrow bands of light filtering in through the thick canopy of leaves overhead. He was sitting on a hard, wooden bench, awkwardly curled into a corner where the side of the wagon protruded, with his feet braced on the running board so he didn't slide.

Memory returned in a rush, and he sat up, gasping as his back cracked in three places as his spine realigned.

"When did we get to a forest?" he asked, turning to look at Emily, who still had her finger raised as if she was planning to poke him again. He eyed that finger until she stuck out her tongue and closed her fist.

"About two hours ago? You've been asleep for about five hours, give or take," Tilly called from where she was climbing down from the seating platform on the other side.

"You okay?" Emily asked. She frowned at him, eyes too shrewd for her age as she studied him. "You never sleep like that when we're on a mission."

"I used a lot of magic last night," Karl replied. "Much more than I normally ever do. I drained my energy reserves. But I'm feeling better now," he added truthfully. The worst of the exhaustion had faded. He didn't feel back to full strength yet, but he would be able to keep up for the rest of the day, and a good night's sleep tonight would clear up the rest. "Did you say we've stopped for lunch?" he asked.

She nodded. "Just long enough to water the horses though. They're passing out cold rations."

"Then let me up. I could use some food."

Emily obediently climbed down, giving Karl room to follow. He stretched again once he was on the ground, working out the last of the ache before heading after Emily to the back of the caravan. Marc was there, passing out traveler's bread, hard and inedible until it was softened with water or tea, which kept it from going bad for months on the road, and he also had a tin of jerky open for people to take from.

Sage and onion exploded on Karl's tongue as he took a bite of jerky, and he held back a groan of pleasure. The jerky was his father's secret recipe, which Char made in large batches for groups leaving the barracks. The hard bread was also Char's, although that was more difficult to tell since most hard bread was the same level of blech and drippy mess once it was softened enough to eat. Ralph walked by as Karl was waiting for his turn with the water skin to douse his bread.

"Looks like we're alone," Ralph called out, speaking toward the wagon. "I'm going to let you guys out."

"Finally!"

The groan was muffled, but the voice recognizable. Karl abandoned his lunch and hurried over in time to see Ralph press on a seemingly random spot on the side of the caravan. A panel on the side popped open, revealing a narrow space about the length of a body. A shuffling sounded, and a moment later Ama squeezed himself out of the space, his cheek rubbing on the ceiling as he'd needed to keep his head turned to fit.

"It's a pressure switch," Ralph explained as he slotted the panel back into place. "I can push the button from this end to open it, but if someone inside doesn't want to be discovered, they can put pressure on the switch from their end and it won't push. I think the engineers who designed this must have been smugglers in a previous life."

Karl nodded and murmured something in answer, but most of his focus was on Ama who was standing hunched over as if he still hurt. Ama was wearing clean clothes and Emily had obviously healed him since he wasn't bleeding everywhere anymore, but he was definitely not in great shape. Even his brown hair looked mottled, as if the lash marks on his back were reflected there.

"I can seal the skin and kill infection, but I'm not strong enough or trained enough to fix the deeper wounds," Emily muttered, a piece of jerky hanging from between her lips.

"He needs a real healer, but we're at least a week out from the border if we can keep this pace," Ralph said, agreeing. Ralph reached up to the arched roof of the wagon and pushed another random spot. A panel a foot square popped open in the overhang for the roof. A moment later a small hand appeared from above the hatch, pushing the panel open along some sort of invisible hinge. The head that followed the hand belonged to a little girl. She had dark hair pulled back into a ragged tail at the base of her neck and equally dark eyes. Karl guessed she was about Emily's age of ten.

She placed both hands flat on the roof as if to lever herself up and out, tensed her shoulders, and then somehow leaped straight up and out of the hatch in one smooth move. She landed easily on the ground at Ralph's side on all fours, looking up at them with a scowl. An image of a kitten, with its back arched and fur on end while spitting angrily, flashed across Karl's imagination. If he had to bet, he would guess she was some sort of cat shifter.

"Lady Ettine, I know our fare is simple, but I promise it is tasty. Please, join us for lunch." Ralph bowed and waved in the direction of where Marc was still supervising lunch.

Lady Ettine stood and dusted off her hands, something regal in the way she managed to look down her nose at Karl. She nodded her thanks to Ralph and headed toward Marc. As she reached where Emily stood, their eyes caught. Both of them looked away sharply, letting out a *humph* as they did. Ettine continued on, while Emily went over to Ama. Clearly there was some history there. Karl shrugged. Either they would work out their difficulties, or they wouldn't. It didn't really matter. Besides, Emily knew better than to let her emotions interfere with a mission so there was no point in Karl worrying or trying to help solve the problem.

"We're close to that pond, right?" Ama asked Ralph, glancing around at their surroundings. All Karl saw were trees and underbrush on either side of the wide dirt path they were following.

"I don't know about 'that pond,' but we're close to Ri Lake," Ralph replied, pointing to their left. "The bank is about a hundred yards that way, and the road follows it to a campsite for our stop tonight."

"They know what I look like; tonight might be too late. Give me five minutes to go wash this out and change my appearance." Ama started hobbling in the direction Ralph had pointed toward.

"I'll come help!" Emily chirped, her voice as bright and cheery as the first robin in the morning—and just as grating. Ettine winced, and suddenly Karl knew why Emily was keeping up her innocent child act despite their being safely away from prying eyes for the moment.

"Whoa there, tiger," Ralph said, dropping a hand on her head to bring her to a halt. "He doesn't need any more healing. Let the man have some space."

Ama was still bent as if it hurt too much to straighten, but he expected to wash himself in that condition. Karl understood why Emily had wanted to help.

"Is there any soap on hand?" Karl asked. "I'll help instead."

"Here!" Marc called, rummaging through the storage area behind him where he had gotten out the lunch food. A moment later he pulled out a cloth and a bar of soap in a travel container. Karl took it with a smile of thanks and hurried after where Ama had vanished into the tree line. Ama wasn't able to move that quickly, so Karl caught up with him easily.

"You don't have to come," Ama said in a low grumble.

Karl shrugged. "I'm mostly trying to keep Emily out of your hair and from using you to antagonize Ettine," Karl explained.

Ama chuckled, then grimaced as he lifted one hand to press against his side. "Not up to laughing just yet. But, yes. Ettine has led a sheltered life cloistered in the often-chilly embrace of Yaroi's deepest traditions. Service. Obedience. Power. Those are the three gods under whose umbrella she was raised. Emily's facade of carefree childishness is probably very confusing for her."

"How do you know Emily is only pretending?" Karl asked, curious since he didn't think Ama had ever met Emily before. Ralph's crew were only in Yaroi for the extraction. As far as Karl knew, they had been a day or so behind Ama's entry into Yari.

"No, I've never met her or you before," Ama said, answering Karl's unspoken question. They reached the bank of a brown lake, the water over-shadowed by thick tree branches overhead. They must be at an inlet of some kind, since it really was little more than a pond, the end of which curved out of view behind more trees another hundred yards away. Ama very slowly lowered himself, kneeling on a dry rock on the bank. He reached for the hem of his shirt and lifted, then paused, his breath hissing out between his teeth.

"Here. Let me," Karl said. He dropped the soap container onto the rock next to Ama and gently gripped the hem of Ama's shirt, lifting it slowly so Ama had time to adjust his arms without causing himself more pain. Lurid red lines crisscrossed Ama's back, angry looking and definitely extremely painful. Like Emily had said, the wounds were closed and clean, but definitely not healed. However, there was no sign of the additional wounds from red magic Karl had managed to heal the previous night. Given enough time, Ama would certainly recover on his own, but getting him to a properly trained healer would speed the process and prevent any lasting damage.

"I've never met you, but I know who you both are," Ama continued as if he needed the conversation to distract him. He fumbled open the soap container and tipped himself forward so his scalp and hair were submerged in the water. Ama's hair looked like he usually kept it cut short, but it must have been a while since he'd had a chance to clip it, so it hung long over his ears. He slowly and stiffly rubbed the soap through his hair, talking as he worked. "Everyone in Toval knows about the three kids Prince Fenwick's pet chef adopted. Braxton filled me in a bit, and I'm perfectly capable of reading between the lines when it comes to political drama. There's no way a kid in Emily's situation turned out to be an empty-headed fop, especially since she's your sister, and I saw what you're capable of last night. You're as qualified a spy for Toval as I am—more capable, since you managed not to get caught in Yari, and I blindly walked right into their trap."

Ama let out a breath and set the soap aside, now using both hands to rinse out the suds. It was hard to tell since the water was darkened by the shadows cast by the surrounding trees, but swirls of brown appeared to be flowing out from Ama's hair like a teabag resting in a cup of water.

"We're not out of the woods yet." Karl paused on those words, glancing around at the forest they were in, then shook his head. "Literally. We're definitely going to need you to get us to Toval again."

Ama chuckled, and the grin he flashed Karl was full of mischief. "Oh, don't worry about my ego. I've been in this game from the moment I was born. I'm mostly avoiding the actual subject I need to talk about." He squeezed the water out of his hair, using his hands to wick any remaining water droplets off his skin. When he slowly levered himself upright again, he shifted so his head was silhouetted in one of the stray beams of sunlight that made it through the trees.

Even darkened by water, the shade of gold of his hair was unmistakable. Only one family in the world had hair that particular shade. Uncle Caro—Prince Caro of Namin, and Uncle Braxton's husband of four years—had hair that exact shade, which belonged to the royal family of Namin exclusively.

"You're—" Karl began, but then Ama tilted his head and his eyes caught the light, and Karl snapped his mouth shut. Karl knew all about how eye color could be indicative of family lineage. He and Emily both had golden-brown eyes that indicated who their shared father was. Ama's eyes were hazel, the exact same shade as Karl's father Fen's, as Braxton's, and the same as every member of the royal family in Toval Karl had ever met. Somehow, Ama had blood from two royal lines from this continent.

Asked a minute earlier, Karl would have been certain Ama's eyes were brown. Karl frowned but helped Ama pull his shirt back over his head and slide his arms into the sleeves.

"How did you change your eye color?" Karl finally asked. That was the only question he felt was polite to ask. The rest was clearly a deep secret Ama no doubt wanted to keep hidden.

"Trade secret," Ama replied, winking cheekily. He staggered back to his feet, Karl helping with a hand on Ama's elbow. The smile faded and Ama sighed. "After this disaster, I somehow doubt I'll have many secrets left. It's not as if I'll be able to work again, not when Yaroi would do almost anything to ensure they can finish punishing me for my crimes. Truthfully, the only way for me to survive is to end the secrecy. So, I guess I'll tell you first."

Ama started walking back toward where the caravan was waiting but stopped after only a few feet to turn and look at Karl. His hazel eyes were serious, far more stoic than Karl had ever seen from him. Even being half dead hadn't made him this sober.

"My mother was Queen Carmillian's youngest sister. The current queen of Namin," Ama clarified. Even though Karl already knew that, Karl let Ama talk. There was no point in interrupting Ama's flow as he forced out what was no doubt a difficult topic. "I am part of the line of royalty who fled Namin after the coup all those years ago. They established a village in Toval, near the border with Namin. About thirty years ago, a young Prince Randolph had a hunting accident in the Spikehorn Mountains. His attendants brought him to the nearest village for healing, but they concealed his identity by claiming he was only a minor noble. He and my mother had a whirlwind romance during the months he was recuperating, and eventually she ended up pregnant with me. Talks of marriage were held off until after my father healed. Except, the moment Randolph was better, he and his retinue left the village without any explanation. My mother didn't survive my birth. I was breech and Randolph had taken our only healer with the ability to help her with him. Aunt Millie raised me instead."

Ama tilted his head back, staring up at the leaf canopy as if he could find answers there.

"Isn't Prince Randolph the one who…" Karl trailed off, uncertain how to say the words to Randolph's son.

"Threw the attempted coup to overthrow the current king of Toval—his older brother? Yes. That's my father. He was married with a five-year-old son at the time he romanced my mother. During the coup, years later, that son was part of the assassination group that attacked Crown Prince Ayer. He died along with just about everyone else in that battle. Ayer barely survived, it was so bloody. Or so I've heard.

"The coup failed and Randolph fled, but his aspirations weren't over. However, he now needed an heir to aid in his claim to the throne, proof that his line would be able to continue leading the country for generations to come, and he remembered he had a kid with my mother. When he fled Etoval after the coup failed, he came to my village hoping to find that child. He had no idea we were Namanese; he only cared about finding his kid. They managed to hide me from him until Braxton arrived and beheaded Randolph."

Ama shook his head and started walking again. Karl stayed close, in case Ama needed him, but it seemed all Ama wanted was to tell his story.

"I was helpless, and I had to watch as other people were hurt in his anger when he found out I wasn't there. I couldn't do anything. And then this handsome prince appeared and slew our enemy. I swore right then I would find a way to repay Braxton, and a few months later I entered his service as a spy.

"I have spent my entire life hiding who I am," Ama continued. "And now, the only way for me to survive to live the rest of my life is to stop hiding." He ran his fingers through his damp hair as if to emphasize the most obvious evidence of that change. "The story I just told you will need to be told and retold over and over until I go crazy."

"Does anyone aside from your aunt know the truth?" Karl asked, wondering if Ama might have more support able to help him.

Ama shrugged. "I wouldn't be surprised if Braxton and Caro know. They certainly suspect. Fen and Char might know, too, since they met me when my aunt retook Namin. I doubt anyone else knows since I've lived in the shadows all this time."

"Couldn't we just dye your hair a different color?" Karl stopped just inside the tree line, the wagon and the waiting group just barely visible through the leaves. "There's no need to announce who you are if we can give you a different appearance instead."

Ama shook his head. "Hair dye won't fool a Yarokian assassin. The only way to avoid death is to convince Yaroi killing me will cause them more problems than they want to deal with. My having ties to two different royal families will go a long way toward persuading them."

"But we first have to get you over the border where that protection is in effect," Karl finished. "Shouldn't we keep your identity hidden until then?"

"I'll just hide in the wagon compartment any time we need to be out of sight," Ama explained. He slipped past Karl and strode back onto the road.

"How did the wolves not smell you in those compartments, by the way?" Karl asked, following Ama.

"That's because the Yarokai aren't as smart as they think," Ralph said, turning around from where he had been helping Marc stow away lunch. Then he caught sight of Ama. "Well, shit."

Chapter Seven

"WE KNEW THEY would have wolves at the gate to do the searches. They have great noses and are very strong, so they can respond to threats," Ama explained as he limped his way into the center of the camp, outwardly oblivious to both Ralph and Marc's dropped jaws. Karl remained at the edge of the path, content to watch everyone's reactions. "Wolfsbane destroys their sense of smell, which they obviously would have noticed, but if you only use subtle hints of wolfsbane in strategic locations they don't realize their sense of smell was affected." Ama stopped walking at the long step up into the driver's seat, tried to lift his foot high enough to reach, and then grimaced and carefully put his foot down again.

"You— You're—" Ralph spluttered.

Ama nodded. "I had to wash out all the dyes, so this is my real appearance. Why do you think Queen Carmillian and Prince Braxton were so anxious to rescue me they sent Karl?" He paused, still grimacing. "I won't be able to walk all the way to the border, especially not at the speed we'll be going. I would prefer not to be confined in the hidden niche the entire time though."

Ralph snapped his mouth shut and shook his head vigorously, as if the force could realign his brain. It apparently worked, since when he focused on Ama again he was only frowning, and his shell-shocked look had faded.

"While we're under the concealment of the trees, you can sit up there. We'll make room for you to sit or lie inside the wagon when we're back out in the plains. Karl, why don't you help him up and take over the reins for the rest of the afternoon?" Ralph clapped his hands, which startled Marc and Tilly back into action.

Karl hurried over, and between himself and Ralph, they managed to lever Ama up into the driver's seat. Karl sat on the bench next to Ama and picked up the reins, realizing as he squeezed the leather straps between his fingers that he had never actually driven a wagon before. Before he could worry about that issue, Tilly appeared at the head of the lead horse, which started following her without Karl needing to actually do anything. Marc and Ralph apparently took rear guard, since Karl couldn't see them as the horses picked up speed. Emily was keeping up her carefree child act, humming softly to herself and occasionally skipping, as she walked with the wagon on Karl's left. To Karl's right, Lady Ettine strode along. Something about the way she walked was slinky. Her hips rolled with every step as if she was used to having more joints than her human body actually held.

"She's a Yarokai," Karl murmured to Ama, gesturing with his chin in Lady Ettine's direction.

Ama nodded, then shook his head. "What do you know about the power structure within Yaroi?" he asked instead of answering.

"The strongest lead, and there's a constant struggle to prove who the strongest actually is," Karl replied slowly as he parsed through his memories of what little he knew about Yaroi. "The royal family are the most powerful, which is why they rule, but there's always a chance someone more powerful could usurp them because that's how their society works. The majority of people in Yaroi shift into some sort of animal form, although there are some who cannot shift at all. And…um…" Karl paused, trying to remember the last part that nearly everyone knew about Yaroi. "Oh, the animal a person shifts into is decided by magic, not family lineage, so parents who shapeshift into rabbits can have a child who shifts into a wolf."

Ama nodded. "That's the gist of how their society works. Sometime between the ages of five and ten, children move from their parents' house to the schools and residences set up for the group of whatever animal they shift into. Within that group, there is a constant power struggle to be the leader, and the leaders are the noble families of the realm. So the alpha of the wolf pack or the head of a clowder might be a duke or marquess, but even the noble titles are based on strength, so the leader of the fluffle will only reach as high as baron since rabbits are considered weak.

"The exception to that is the royal family. None of them ever join a herd or pack. They're strong, we know that, or they wouldn't be the rulers of Yaroi, but we don't know much more about their shape-shifting abilities. They keep the secret of their royal magic closely guarded from the rest of the world. What we do know, from Queen Trina, is the royal family are subject to similar internal power struggles. Queen Trina was sent away to Toval as a marriage prospect because she didn't have Yaroi's royal magic, but also because she was born without the ability to shift forms. She has no animal nature inside."

The marriage restrictions within the royal families of the continent were common knowledge. If a prince or princess could wield the royal magic, they remained home. Any children born without the royal magic became fodder for marriage contracts with foreign nations because they could be sent away. Queen Trina's marriage to the king of Toval had solidified trade agreements between Yaroi and Toval. All four of their children had the royal magic of Toval so had remained in Toval.

"What you're saying is the Yaroi royal family takes the royal marriage issue to another level," Karl said, focused on the part Ama had explained about Queen Trina not being able to shift forms at all. "They only allow children with no shifting ability whatsoever to leave Yaroi as marriage prospects?"

Ama nodded. "Exactly. Which brings up the question of what happens to the princesses and princes who are not born with the royal magic but can shift forms."

"I'm assuming it's not good," Karl replied, frowning.

"My fiancé was chosen for me this year," Lady Ettine suddenly cut in, her eyes sharp and shrewd, far too shrewd for a ten-year-old. "Earl Blackenwater controls significant territory to the west along the mountain border with Zafindere. He's over fifty years old, and his first three wives did not survive, although no one asked any questions about what happened to them. I was to be married to him next month. I wrote to my dear aunt in Toval, asking for her advice, and she sent Ama."

"This is Princess Melody Ettine Leon Ealdwulf Dracen Yarotai, a cat shifter of some sort who did not inherit the royal magic, and I was tasked with kidnapping her and bringing her to Toval," Ama added, his carefree grin back in place. He liked shocking people, Karl realized, and that childlike grin was oddly cute below eyes that were serious and said he understood the gravity of the situation they were in despite joking about it.

"We're traveling through the middle of nowhere in Yaroi with two members of royalty, one of whom is running away from home. This is going to go well, I can tell," Karl groused, shifting on the uncomfortable bench, unwilling to let his brain focus on where Lady Ettine was supposed to end up. He was too disgusted.

Ama gave him a sharp look that was part admonishment and part curiosity. "You do know that even though you weren't officially adopted by Prince Fenwick, you're listed everywhere as his son? We technically have three members of royalty in this caravan."

"And that is why we're going to run our way through Yaroi and across that border, before Yaroi realizes just who we are," Ralph added, appearing next to Emily on Karl's left.

It was also why Ralph was here, Karl added mentally as the realization dawned. Ralph was usually Char's bodyguard but was acclaimed as one of the best swordsmen in the entirety of Toval. If Toval wanted to protect someone, sending Ralph was a great idea. Karl would also bet Marc and Tilly were equally strong. And, despite being only ten, Emily was very good with a blade as well. This was a miniature war band.

Not being officially adopted by Fen wasn't a sore spot for Karl. Most people, particularly courtiers, thought it would be and tended to try poking at that perceived wound first. When he was younger, Karl had been confused by them. He completely understood why Fen couldn't adopt him and definitely appreciated Fen still taking on the role of second father anyway, so it made zero sense to Karl why people thought needling him about it would garner any sort of reaction out of him. These days, Karl knew they were jealous. Thankfully, since Karl had spent most of his time in a kitchen before heading off to Timmonsville for two years, he didn't have to interact with them much.

Still, apparently being unofficially adopted was enough to make him one of the problems Ralph needed to keep an eye on. Karl suppressed a sigh. Also, Karl realized in dawning horror as the thought came to him, if they were caught and Yaroi found out the royalty of two separate nations was complicit in kidnapping their princess… He couldn't complete that horrifying thought even in his own head. It did explain why Ama's punishment had been so vile, his body literally rotting to death after they finished torturing him, if Ama was the one who helped Lady Ettine escape from the palace in Yari. Karl had no idea how Ama had managed that, but Karl was glad Braxton had diverted him into Yari to help save Ama. Even if it meant three members of royalty were relying on Ralph to get them home safely.

Ralph had dropped back again, and Lady Ettine was walking with Tilly. Karl looked at Ama, ready to pepper him with all his questions, but closed his mouth without saying anything. Ama was asleep, his chin resting on his chest, just above where his arms were crossed. He looked uncomfortable, but completely exhausted, so Karl let him sleep.

The wagon rocked as they went over a rough patch of roots, tilting slightly to the left. The movement was normal for a wagon on a dirt road in the middle of a forest; nothing extreme or dangerous for Karl to notice or care about. But, as the wagon settled back down Ama's body shifted with the motion and his head came to rest on Karl's shoulder. His breaths puffed against Karl's neck, warm and somehow soothing. Karl froze in place for a long moment, his attention completely focused on the top of that head of blond hair, filling his vision and somehow sending curling waves of contentment through Karl's body.

He barely knew Ama. Karl would absolutely be the first to say so, and yet, he still really, really liked having Ama using him for a pillow. Some inner part of himself was figuratively purring in contentment. Unfortunately, this wasn't the time or place to be having such feelings. Trying to move quickly through a dangerous situation was not the right moment to be developing a crush, so Karl stuffed those feelings back down.

Still, he couldn't leave Ama with his cheek pressed to the boniest part of Karl's shoulder. Trying not to blush, and definitely hoping Ralph or Emily weren't close enough to notice, Karl shifted slightly so Ama's head fit better into the crook of his shoulder. Maybe once they were back in Toval, he could let his feelings loose again, and see whether Ama was interested, in return, but for now Karl let out a breath and turned to look at where the horses he was supposed to be driving were headed.

They continued on, heading south and following the river, as the sun slowly began to dip in the western horizon. And Ama's closeness kept Karl warm the entire way.

Chapter Eight

"I KNOW WE said we hired you to cook, but Char outfitted us with more than enough supplies before we left," Ralph explained to Karl as they all worked to set up camp for the night. They had pulled the caravan to the side of a man-made clearing, no doubt created exactly for the purpose they were using it for since the center of the clearing already had a stone-lined firepit waiting for them.

"More than just his jerky?" Karl asked, holding a box Marc had handed him while Marc rifled through its contents.

"He gave us a ton of these!" Marc said, triumphantly holding up a bag with a secure tie at the top. Karl immediately recognized it, and a nostalgic smile lifted his lips slightly. He had spent far too much time in the kitchen chopping and mixing, then watching while Char used his magic to dry the ingredients, before they packed everything away in those food-safe bags. Char's travel soups and stews lasted for months in their dried form and just required boiling water and ten to twenty minutes of simmering to be edible again. The magically dried ingredients would reconstitute in the boiling water and then the flavors melded into something delicious.

"Do you have bread or yeast or something I can use to make a side dish?" Karl asked. Ralph took the bag from Marc, and Marc took the box from Karl, who followed Ralph to where Tilly was feeding sticks to the lit kindling in the fire pit. They had a while before the fire was hot enough to boil water.

Unfortunately, Ralph shook his head. "We didn't get word you would be landing in Yaroi rather than your original plan of sailing through the Strait and landing in Toval until just before we crossed the border into Yaroi and we had to cut off communication. If I had known when we were packing we were extracting you too, I promise our wagon would have been stuffed to the brim with flour and yeast and everything you might need to make bread out here. I've been on a couple tours where Char was able to bake, so I definitely know what I'm missing out on," Ralph added, whining, even though he was grinning to show he was teasing too.

Karl let out a heavy sigh and shook his head, trying to look disappointed. "That's too bad. I guess you'll have to wait until we're back home to see how much better my baking has gotten in the last two years."

"Ugh! That's forever from now!" Ralph joked back. They both started laughing, only calming down when Emily dropped some logs next to the fire for Tilly to use once the kindling was going, then gave them a look that said: "Why am I working so hard when you're just standing around?" Karl swallowed down another snicker and went to find the tripod to hang a pot from over the fire, so they would be ready to start cooking as soon as Emily's logs were burning.

Dinner ended up being Char's corn chowder, heavy on the potato and celery, with red bell peppers for color and nutrients. Scents of rich onion and thyme bathed Karl's face as he buried his nose in the billowing steam. The dining hall at Timmonsville was run by culinary students, sometimes with mixed results in what they had on offer each meal. Needless to say, Karl had greatly missed Char's cooking, which was consistently delicious every day. Even this slightly watery version of Char's chowder—powdered milk and cream never reconstituted perfectly no matter how well Char's magic dried it—made a lump form in Karl's throat. He forced that lump away, swallowing hard and trying to think of things other than being homesick, then took his first sip.

Slightly watery, exactly as he had feared—the best way to reconstitute this particular soup was probably in boiled milk rather than water, which they weren't going to get out here—but the abundance of corn kernels and the bite-sized cubes of potato were perfectly soft and helped soothe the rumbling gremlins in his stomach.

"Needs bread," Karl grumbled in between mouthfuls. A crusty roll, hard on the outside, but soft on the inside, would be perfect for sopping up broth and filling the holes in his stomach the potato just couldn't fill.

Ralph laughed. "Now you sound exactly like Char. Unfortunately, you'll probably think the same thing for all the rest of our meals on this trip. It's a different soup or stew every night. I know Char was looking for a way to equip us with fresh bread to go with each. It's really too bad the only bread suitable for travel is that hard crap. You put one of those lumps of coal in a soup like this, and you'll ruin the soup."

Char would probably be able to take one of those "lumps of coal" and turn it into something spectacular, using only what was available in this camp, but Karl wasn't that talented. Yeast spoke to him through his magic, and he had studied ratios of dry to wet ingredients and things like eggs, bananas, baking powder, and baking soda for rising alternatives, but he wasn't a Musen by blood. Karl didn't have that extra spark inside that made his food amazing like Char did; he only had a fanatic's level of interest.

Thankfully, even without the bread, the chowder was delicious and filling. When he was done, Karl helped them clean up, washing the pot and bowls alongside Marc at the bank of Ri Lake, which wasn't too far from the campsite.

"Right—" Ralph was in the middle of speaking when Karl returned to the camp, his arms full of cleaned dishes. "—Ama, Lady Ettine, I'm afraid the safest place for you tonight is back in your hidey holes, just in case someone tries to sneak into camp to investigate us. I know it's uncomfortable, but we have to make do until we're able to cross the border," he added when Lady Ettine frowned. "A little discomfort now, and I promise you, as soon as we reach Toval, you'll get the treatment you deserve for your station."

"I understand, and I'm not ungrateful," Lady Ettine replied, still frowning. "But…"

"We'll be sleeping on hard wood, which means we won't be doing much sleeping," Ama grumbled. "I have a feeling we'll need to get used to it, my lady. Once we leave this forest, I suspect we'll need to be hidden for the duration of our journey across the Eiri Plains."

Ralph grunted his agreement. "Too many opportunities to be spotted out there. You'll be able to walk around at twilight and dawn when the light is hardest for any watchers to see us, but otherwise you'll have to be tucked away."

"I will endure," Lady Ettine said, her frown turning stoic. "A few days of uncomfortable confinement is certainly better than the lifetime of torture my parents were about to subject me to. Please give me a lift up."

Ralph hurried over and bent to one knee, letting her step onto the raised knee and use his shoulder for balance before she lifted herself up onto the wagon roof and into the opening. Ama waited by his own hatch. He looked wan in the firelight, hunched over and exhausted, despite sleeping most of the afternoon. Ralph and Marc together had to bodily lift him up into the crawl space—his arms gave out when he tried himself.

They left the doors open as the rest of the group laid out bedrolls in the shadow of the wagon, only sealing Ama and Lady Ettine in at the last minute. Karl settled into his bedroll, frowning up at where Ama was tucked away.

Ama really hadn't looked good, sick and weak. All that fire, his flame of personality Karl remembered from when they were escaping Yari's torture arena, was absent. Emily might have sealed the flesh wounds, but there was definitely some internal damage she didn't have the power or training to heal. Never mind getting Lady Ettine to safety, they needed to get across the border in order to get Ama to a healer.

Karl slowly slid into sleep, his body dragging him down into oblivion mid-worry, but he kept waking up. The ground was uncomfortable. Every stray noise—the wind blowing through the leaves, the pop of wood in the banked fire, Marc snoring lightly—had him jolting awake, his eyes flying open and adrenaline pumping. When he did sleep, he dreamed of terrible things: Finding Ama dead on that whipping cross and not being able to save him. Opening the hatch to Ama's hiding spot in the morning to find a rotting corpse.

When the barest hint of light peeked through the trees and Ralph grunted and rolled to his feet, Karl was all too glad to abandon that fitful cycle. He helped pass out more of Char's jerky for breakfast, and they made a quick pot of tea on the fire's embers, but they didn't hang around for long. Marc and Ralph got Ama out of his hiding compartment and up onto the bench, Marc climbing up for his turn sitting. They put out the fire, packed up any remaining debris from the campsite, and headed out.

Karl walked next to the wagon, below where Ama sat. Ama hadn't been able to help much, barely supporting his own weight as Marc and Ralph levered him up there, and Karl was worried he might fall. He spent the entire day paying more attention to Ama's every movement than where he placed his own feet, which led to him tripping over protruding roots and stones in the path more than once. Marc switched with Lady Ettine after lunch, which Ama slept through.

And they walked. On and on, the sunlight dappling the ground as it filtered through the leaves overhead. Night fell as they reached another campsite along the banks of Ri Lake. Dinner that night was vegetable soup. Beef and mushroom stock that sang on Karl's tongue, all kinds of vegetables cut into exacting cubes, and tiny little squares of pasta, and every spoonful sank like a stone in Karl's stomach. Ama barely got down a few bites. Despite sleeping all day, he looked exhausted.

"Drink the broth, at least," Ralph told Ama, holding the bowl for him since Ama's hands were shaking. "You need the liquids." Ama squeezed his eyes shut and then nodded, opening his mouth when Ralph tipped the bowl for him and drinking directly from the side.

Karl barely slept that night, worries jolting him awake, certain every noise was Ama crying out for help. In the morning, he helped Ralph get

Ama down from the compartment. Ama's skin was clammy and hot. He definitely had a fever. Ralph forced him to drink two cups of tea, and then rather than putting him up on the bench, they tucked Ama back into the compartment again. Ralph rigged the door so it remained open a crack so Ama could have fresh air, and they continued on.

They stopped to rest late afternoon, as the forest was thinning. Long, brown grass waving in the wind was visible through the trees.

"From here on, we'll be out in the open. Sorry, my lady, but this is where we'll need to hide you away again."

Lady Ettine sighed, but nodded, accepting Ralph's help to climb back up into her hiding spot. Ralph closed Ama's door too, and they rolled on.

The forest ended abruptly. One moment they were in the forest, and the next they stepped out into vast prairies. The grass Karl had only glimpsed before stretched out ahead of them for miles, an endless expanse brown in the early spring, even with the sun blazing overhead. The path was cut into the ground in grooves from years of wagons traveling on it in four parallel lines: two for the wagons heading to Toval, and two for the wagons headed into the forest. They were able to move faster now, and Karl found himself speed walking for the rest of the afternoon. When they stopped for the night at twilight, simply halting right in the path, Karl's legs ached, but he had definitely recovered from his ordeal. Ama, on the other hand, hadn't improved at all.

Their fire was in the center of the path, between the two sets of parallel lines. Ralph had to hold Ama up to eat. Tonight's soup was chicken, Char's wake-you-up-from-the-dead chicken stock with chunks of carrot, parsnip, and celery mixed with chicken pieces and more of those tiny pasta squares. Ralph got Ama to drink most of the broth, but Ama didn't open his eyes the entire time. He was deteriorating swiftly.

Marc and Emily ate hidden inside the wagon, so anyone who might be watching wouldn't suddenly see more people walking around the wagon than expected, so Ralph's voice was a little louder than usual when he spoke so they could hear.

"We've got good moonlight and a straight path. Let's give the horses a few more minutes to rest and see if we can't make up some time tonight." He pressed a hand to Ama's forehead and grimaced. "We'll sleep in shifts. Emily and Tilly, you're up on the bench. Marc, you'll sleep in the wagon. Karl and I will take first shift walking. We'll swap at midnight when we rest the horses again."

They finished dinner and got everything cleaned and put away. Ama and Lady Ettine returned to their compartments and the rest of the group went to where Ralph had directed. Ralph took the front, one hand on the lead horse's bridle to guide them along. Karl took the back of the wagon, trying to keep an eye out for anything attempting to sneak up on them from behind. Their pace was slightly slower in the dark, but thanks to the marked road and the three-quarter moon overhead, they still made good time. Karl ended up on the bench when they swapped at midnight, Ralph in the wagon, while Tilly, Marc, and Emily took their turns walking. Around two in the morning, tilled fields suddenly interrupted the prairie, the dirt freshly turned and ready for spring planting. Farther afield were fenced pastures with cows and sheep. About an hour later, they clattered through a small hamlet, the houses dark and only a dog barking indicating anyone else was alive. The night felt endless, like some sort of magical loop in time. Just them and the town, silvered in the moonlight so it looked surreal. Past the town were more fields, and then the prairie returned, the stalks of grass waving hypnotically in the gentle breeze. Karl couldn't sleep, but his consciousness drifted, hovering in that awkward space between asleep and awake as if he couldn't quite decide which way to fall.

At dawn they stopped for an hour. Karl went through the motions of helping to pass out jerky, but his fingers moved without any seeming involvement of his brain, almost as if he were a zombie. They didn't bother with a fire, drinking water from their stores along with the rations. Ralph got Ama to drink a little, but that was all. Once the horses were cooled down, fed, and watered, they headed out again. Karl took his turn walking, and the movement energized him a bit, but he still felt disconnected from reality. Endless prairie passed on either side. Karl could have been walking in place, each step seemingly bringing him no closer to anywhere. A surge of relief ran through him when the prairie ended, again replaced by cultivated fields and pastures, except, half of Karl was convinced this was the same village they had passed through the previous night, and they were simply walking in circles.

They stopped in the town square, where Ralph bartered for access to their well and for a couple loaves of fresh bread. Aside from the person Ralph spoke with, the rest of the villagers gave them a wide berth. Mothers steered children away and men glared when they passed. Once the horses were watered and they had eaten some of the bread, they continued onward. Ralph passed some bread and jerky up to Lady Ettine once they were back into the prairie, and they stopped again briefly at noon to swap who was walking versus who was resting, but that was it for excitement the rest of that morning.

"We're going to have to stop for a few hours tonight," Ralph said, grunting. He had joined Karl up on the bench, giving Tilly the back of the wagon for an extended rest. Marc was up front and Emily covered their rear. "Horses won't make it if we don't."

"How much farther until we reach the border?" Karl asked.

Ralph grimaced. "Between our fast pace and not stopping last night, we've probably cut at least a day, day and a half off the route, so it's hard to say exactly. Since we're forced to stop tonight, perhaps a little after lunch tomorrow? That's my best estimate."

Karl lowered his voice just in case anyone was around to overhear. "How far past the border before we reach a healer?"

Ralph glanced over his shoulder at the wagon where Ama was hidden away, also lowering his voice. "Under an hour. Reinforcements are supposed to be waiting five miles from the border—far enough away they won't arouse suspicion, but close enough to support us. As soon as we're over the river, we'll make a sprint for them."

Ama would have to survive until then. Emily might not be able to heal him, but perhaps she could give Ama a little extra strength to help him get through the next twenty-four hours. If everything went as planned, Ama would be with a qualified healer soon… If.

Karl forced back his pessimistic thoughts. Ama was ill, but he knew he was safe and all he had to do was hang on until they could get him to help. That hope would bolster Ama, would keep him fighting. And that hope would also keep Karl from worrying. At least, that was what Karl told himself as firmly as possible as the hours passed and the sun began to sink into the horizon.

They made camp that night, their bedrolls next to the wagon and the fire in the middle of the road. The horses ate and drank, then promptly went to sleep, even more exhausted than Karl. They had no choice but to let the horses rest.

Ama didn't open his eyes when Ralph and Marc carefully pulled him free, his head lolling and limp. His breathing came in short pants, and his face was flushed.

"We need to get fluids in him," Ralph muttered, eying the beef stew bubbling in the pot hanging from the tripod over the fire. There was good broth in there with a ton of nutrients, and plenty of water in their water skins, but Ama had to be conscious enough to swallow.

"Can you do anything for him?" Karl asked Emily.

"I can't make him any worse," Emily replied, heading over to where Ralph was cradling Ama. Her hands glowed green as she pressed them to Ama's chest and frowned in concentration. Karl stirred the stew as he watched, heart thudding. At least five minutes passed with nothing happening. Tilly and Marc finished setting up camp, and Lady Ettine remained hidden until Emily could vanish from view, but her hatch was open while she waited. Finally, Ama's eyelids fluttered, and he let out a soft groan.

Emily's knees gave out and she landed on her butt in the dirt, but she was grinning. "I was able to reduce the fever a bit and some of the swelling," she explained. "I still can't fix what's causing all that," she added with a scowl, "but he should be able to eat and rest a bit better until the symptoms flare up again."

Emily had bought Ama a bit more time, which was really all they needed if Ralph was correct and reinforcements were just over the border. Karl quickly filled a bowl with only broth and brought it over for Ama to eat before he fell asleep again.

"Drink all of this," Ralph instructed, taking the bowl from Karl with a nod of thanks. "And more water. The water skin you had with you is still mostly full, so you definitely haven't had enough to drink today."

Ama didn't respond. His eyes were open, but they weren't really focused on anything. He wasn't actually awake, just conscious. Karl took the bowl back from Ralph so Ralph could hold Ama steady while Karl carefully tipped the contents into Ama's mouth. Ama swallowed automatically. It wasn't long before the bowl was empty, and they moved on to feeding Ama plain water.

"You have to drink." Karl only realized he was murmuring that phrase over and over again to Ama when Ralph smirked at him, but Karl didn't stop. It didn't matter if Ama spent the rest of the night finding somewhere to pee, he needed the liquids to combat the fever. Only when Ama let out an indistinct sound of protest and turned his head away did Karl put the water skin down. Ralph settled Ama into one of the bedrolls, covering him tightly in the warm fabric.

"This way he'll get some fresh air," Ralph explained as he stood. He gripped Karl on the shoulder and turned them both back toward the fire. "Now it's our turn to eat and get some rest. If the horses recover enough, I would like to leave not long after midnight."

Karl obeyed, filling a bowl of stew for himself before stepping to the side so Ralph could get some too. Beef stock with a tomato base, thick cubes of stewing beef, potatoes, carrots, onions, and whatever other vegetables Char had on hand—this was one of the meals Char served in the coldest parts of winter when the soldiers who ate in his mess hall most needed a stick-to-your-ribs shot of warmth. Karl savored every bite, the sharp tang of bay and basil mixing perfectly with all the other flavors. When Char could get it, his secret ingredient was okra to help thicken the stew, but Karl thought this version was made with dried peas as thickener instead.

The peas probably powdered better for transport in a travel bag under Char's magic than the okra. At the mess hall, Char served this with his garlic bread dripping with butter and spices, which had a crunchy crust and soft inside perfect for sopping up any remaining liquid in the bowl.

"Needs garlic bread," Karl muttered.

Tilly heard him and let out a laugh. "Oh, yeah. Chef Char's garlic bread." She made a yum sound, her eyes and mouth closed tight in what looked like remembered ecstasy, but then she suddenly spun to look at Ralph. "Do we have any more of that bread we bought in that village?"

Ralph's eyes lit up. "We do. We don't have butter or garlic, but at least we can have bread. Marc! Where's that bread gone?"

Marc was inside the wagon with Emily, staying hidden while Ama and Lady Ettine were out, but he still yelled back a moment later. "Got a whole loaf and a half in here. Let me cut some slices for everyone."

Karl got two slices of bread only starting to go stale, which added to the crunch and made it perfect for sopping up broth. Without the garlic and butter, the taste profile wasn't nearly as good, but using the bread to sop up the dregs of broth in his bowl was still extremely satisfying. Karl licked his fingers when he was done, sighing happily.

Karl helped with the cleanup and then crawled into a bedroll. He couldn't think clearly enough to remember how long it had been since he had actually slept properly. The ship from Timmonsville to Yari had been cramped, uncomfortable, and smelly. He hadn't slept then. The next night was when he had rescued Ama, and Karl had gotten only a few hours' sleep. He had slept in the wagon that morning, but that was more due to magic exhaustion than getting actual rest. He certainly hadn't slept well the last few nights. A week, maybe? Had he really been traveling that long? Karl tried to get his brain to engage and got nothing. He rolled over and only then realized he was next to Ama.

Beneath his tan, Ama's skin was bleached out, pale and clammy with massive dark circles under his eyes. None of the vivacity Karl remembered from after Ama's rescue remained, only this shell of sickness. Whatever Emily had done to help was already wearing off. Still, being close like this, able to hear Ama's breathing and see his chest moving beneath the bedroll, was somehow relaxing. Karl's eyes slid closed, and he drifted off to sleep, comforted by the lullaby of Ama nearby.

Chapter Nine

KARL'S INNER SENSES, far too attuned to someone leaning over him in his sleep, jolted him awake. He gasped, trying to stem the instinctive panic, and sat up.

"Sorry, kid!" Ralph said, his tone slow and soothing. "I forgot. It's just me. You're safe."

Karl wiped sweat off his forehead and purposely slowed his panting, breathing in through his nose and out his mouth the way he knew worked to get his heart to stop thudding frantically in his chest. He didn't honestly remember what had happened when he was a kid that now caused him to absolutely freak out whenever someone leaned over him like Ralph had just accidentally done. The circumstances of his birth were a massive question mark. Karl was pretty certain who his father was but had zero idea about his mother. Soon after his birth, he had been sent to a special home meant to house and hide away bastard children of Toval's nobility. He had met his adoptive brother Shan there, and a few years later, Emily joined them. And then one of the local gangs got too interested in how a peasant family always seemed to have extra money for food and such when the man and woman who ran the facility never seemed to work. The gang had attacked, hoping to get their hands on some of that money, but instead destroyed the house and sent the inhabitants scattering to safety.

Karl didn't know where anyone else had ended up, nor whether the adults had survived. In the end, he, Shan, and Emily had found a hidey-hole for themselves up until the day Karl had gotten caught trying to pickpocket Jensen, one of the leaders of the Royal Forces. Karl firmly believed his life had actually started the day he walked into the barracks where the Royal Forces were housed. Everything before that was just a hiccup—except when someone leaned over him and his body reacted without any input from his brain.

"Horses are awake and eating, so we're packing. It's about one in the morning," Ralph continued, knowing that talking to Karl was the best way to bring him out of that instinctive panic. "I'm hoping to get Ama to drink some more before we have to hide him away again, if you want to help?"

Focusing on Ama was enough to fight off the last dregs of panic. Karl climbed out of his bedroll and grabbed a nearby water skin. While Ralph held Ama upright, his head high, Karl carefully trickled water into Ama's mouth. Ama did swallow some of it, but most of the water trickled back out, sliding between his lips to splash on the ground.

"We're almost there," Karl whispered into Ama's ear, hoping Ama could hear and understand. "Just hang on a little longer."

They got Ama tucked back into his hiding spot and the horses hooked to the wagon, and they were off. Karl walked to the side of the wagon, close to the hatch, not that he could do anything for Ama when they were moving like this, but it made him feel better all the same. He only hoped Ama might sense him out here and find some comfort.

Hours went by as the miles passed under Karl's feet. The moon set long before the sun rose, but the path was clear even in the darkness, the wagon's wheels firm in the ruts. The horses didn't seem to be particularly pleased about moving in the dark, grunting and biting at the bits in their mouths, but under Tilly's urging, they kept walking. Finally, the barest hints of light began to grow on the horizon to their left. They were able to move faster then, picking up their pace as the first sliver of sun crested over the prairie grass, lighting their way. Once the sun was fully visible, around what Karl estimated to be six o'clock, Ralph called a halt.

"Let's have a quick breakfast," Ralph called, and Marc scrambled to the back of the wagon to go dig out the jerky and some oats for the horses. Karl headed to Ama's hatch, but something made him pause, his fingers on the release button. The hairs on the back of his neck were standing up. He stepped away, looking around into the grass.

The sunlight burnished the prairie to a beautiful shade of gold, glittering as the morning dew began to evaporate. Everything looked peaceful, and yet his instincts, honed by his years on the streets and sharpened by his time with the Royal Forces, said otherwise.

"What is it?" Ralph asked, stopping at Karl's side. His hand drifted to his side, but he grimaced when he only found his belt knife. In his role as a merchant, he couldn't openly wear his sword, but Karl had a feeling it was hidden somewhere on the wagon within easy reach.

"I don't—" Something flashed out of the corner of Karl's eye, and he spun to look. High, up in the sky, something shiny reflected against the sun, like metal soaring through the air.

Karl squinted, trying to figure out what the heck was up there. Whatever it was turned and banked like a raptor, but no bird Karl had ever heard of came in metallic colors. Karl also thought it was far too large to be a mere bird. Maybe someone was flying a kite…out in the middle of nowhere in Yaroi. Not likely. He used one hand to shade his eyes from the rising sun, but that didn't help either. If Karl wasn't mistaken, whatever it was, it was getting closer. And bigger.

"Shit," Ralph swore.

Karl glanced at Ralph briefly, unwilling to take his eyes off the incoming thing. Ralph's face had gone pale, and he hurried past Karl to the wagon, from which he opened a small door and pulled out a sword.

"What is it?" Karl asked, looking back to the sky. He could make out some details now. It was silver, with a pair of long wings and a long neck. Possibly there were some spikes on its head and along its back, or it was wearing some sort or armor. Actually, now that Karl thought about it, maybe it was a type of raptor wearing armor. Yaroi probably had bird shapeshifters, so giving them protection while in flight wouldn't be too strange.

"That," Ralph forced out, sounding like he was being strangled by the words, "is one of the dragons of Yaroi."

"A dragon?" Karl gasped out. "Aren't those just in fairy tales?"

Ralph opened his mouth to respond, but before he could say anything a thump came from over their heads, from the roof of the wagon.

"Let me out! Let me out right now!" Lady Ettine demanded, thumping on the wagon again.

"My lady, it's dangerous right now," Ralph called back, his gaze still focused on the incoming dragon.

"I said, let me out!"

Ralph grimaced, but still reached up to press the hidden lever that opened Lady Ettine's compartment door. She tumbled gracelessly into the path below and sprang to her feet, dashing out from under the wagon overhang to look at the dragon swooping in from above. Suddenly, she lifted one hand into the air and waved.

"What the—" Ralph cut himself off before he could swear again. He stomped in her direction, but then froze in place when she cupped her hands over her mouth and yelled.

"Brother! Brother, I'm here!"

"Weren't we helping her run away from her family?" Marc muttered as he abandoned the back of the wagon to join Ralph and Karl in staring incredulously at her. Emily came over as well, scowling fiercely at Lady Ettine in the first break of her established character she had allowed the entire trip. No one would mistake her for the happy-go-lucky child she had been pretending to be with an expression like that on her face—as if she could easily kill Lady Ettine, hide her body, and not lose any sleep over it. Tilly was over by the horses, but kept looking over at Ralph, awaiting further instructions.

"I'm more curious about why she's yelling "brother" at a frickin dragon," Ralph replied. He was still holding his sword, but his hands were relaxed.

The dragon banked overhead, turning and swooping lower, moving downwind, Karl realized, when the horses didn't make any sounds of alarm. The dragon's scales were silver, shot through with golden streaks like lightning bolts. The tips of its horns, and where the scales ended on all four paws, the end of its tail, and its snout, were all fully gold. The dragon was easily double the size of the wagon, and it cast a very long shadow in the light of the rising sun as it back-winged for landing. Half a second before the claws touched the ground, a golden shimmer flowed over the dragon. The dragon vanished, replaced by a human man.

Golden magic! Karl gasped. That was definitely golden magic. The only people who could use golden magic were the royal families. No one knew what Yaroi's royal magic consisted of. They kept it so secret Karl had heard even Queen Trina hadn't known. If they could shapeshift into mythical dragons, Karl could understand why they kept it quiet.

At first glance he appeared ordinary enough, especially in his simple brown pants with his white shirt tucked in at the waist, but he definitely looked too much like Lady Ettine to actually be ordinary. They shared the same black hair and dark eyes, but he was older than her, around Karl's age, and a lot taller. He had to be at least six feet.

"Don't stop!" he yelled, striding forward. "I tried to distract the guard with evidence that she boarded a ship, but they somehow unraveled that already and sent a full company after you! They're barely half a day's gallop behind you!"

Ralph swore again, already spinning to the rest of their group. "Let's go!" he snapped out.

A flurry of movement erupted. Everything was put away again quickly, and the wagon was moving forward within seconds. Tilly and Emily rode astride the front horses, Karl and Ralph got seats on the driving platform, and Marc and the dragon both hung off the side of the wagon, their feet on the step up to the driver's area. Lady Ettine was tucked back away in her compartment, and Karl hadn't had time to check on Ama, but he was tucked away too. And the wagon *moved*.

If Karl thought they had been traveling fast before, he was wrong. They flew down the path, the wheels rattling in the grooves so much Karl had to stiffen his neck to keep from getting whiplash.

"Who are you, exactly?" Ralph asked.

Karl wouldn't have dared open his mouth, too afraid they would hit a bump and he would bite his tongue. That didn't seem to deter Ralph or the dragon, who responded with an easy shrug.

"You may call me Lyric," the dragon replied. "I am Melody—ah, Lady Ettine's—older brother and her coconspirator in her escape plan. I believe I was betrayed and my part in her escape was revealed to my uncle, King Rikash. I will aid you in getting across the border, and I hope I might claim the same asylum as Melody."

"I would think something can be arranged, but I will leave decisions like that to Their Majesties," Ralph said. "I know any help getting us through this final checkpoint and into Toval would be much appreciated."

"I'll do my best," Lyric replied, something cheeky in the sideways twist of a grin he shot them.

They lapsed into silence. Karl focused on the road ahead while trying not to worry about how close their pursuers were behind them. He couldn't see anything, not even a dust cloud to indicate anyone might be there, but he had a feeling Lyric wouldn't have revealed himself the way he had if the situation wasn't dire. Divulging the secret of Yaroi's royal magic couldn't have come lightly to him, after all.

They had to slow the horses to a walk to rest them, and Tilly and Marc dashed around getting water and food to all the horses and humans. After a few miles, they picked up the pace again, although not as fast as the horses were tiring. Ralph glanced at the angle of the sun every few minutes, no doubt gauging how far they had traveled versus how far they still had to go.

Finally, Ralph nodded to himself. "Let's slow up!" he called out. Tilly waved a hand in acknowledgement and the horses slowed to a walk. "Rub them down," Ralph added. "I don't want to look like we're in any kind of hurry when we get to the border."

Tilly and Marc set about the horses with brushes and water, cooling them down and removing any traces of lather or sweat. Emily had to dismount to walk, and Karl joined her, letting Lyric take his seat.

Even with both feet solidly on the ground, Karl's bones still felt like they were vibrating, jostling and bouncing around under his skin as if he were still on the cart. His neck was aching from holding it stiff for so long, but that thankfully started smoothing out as he stretched his body into a walk. Eventually the internal rattling faded as well, although that took a lot longer. They picked up the pace a touch once the horses were ready, just enough to be faster than walking but nowhere close to their headlong pace from earlier, so the miles passed by quickly underfoot.

Karl kept glancing behind, waiting to see that telltale cloud of dust, which would indicate someone was coming, but he didn't see anything. He faced forward again as they reached the top of a rise just in time to see their destination appear below.

The Eiroi River sparkled under the glow of the midmorning sun, a glittering ribbon cutting through eerily similar plains on either side. At the bottom of the rise, their last obstacle awaited. A large stone bridge crossed the river, which even from this distance looked too wide, deep, and fast flowing to ford. A small guardhouse graced each side of the bridge, and as their wagon came into view, guards came out of each.

Karl glanced over at Lyric, but he was smiling genially as if this was just a normal day for him. The others were professionals trained to bluff their way through. Only Karl appeared to be the weak link, but he had managed to get out of Yari, so he could do this too. He hoped.

Chapter Ten

"HALT!" ONE OF the guards barked out as the wagon reached them. Tilly stopped the horses, and Ralph jumped down from the steering bench and approached the guards, his hands outheld at his sides to show he was unarmed.

"Good morning," Ralph called out, a genial smile on his face. "Would you like to see our papers? We've traveled from Yari."

The guards didn't relax, all six of them frowning. The one who had called out earlier stepped up to Ralph, one hand on the sword hilt at his hip.

"Border's closed. Turn around and return to Yari."

"Good sir, we cannot afford to turn around. Money is not made on the road, after all." Ralph pressed one hand to his chest to show his sincerity, bowing slightly.

"Border's closed," the guard repeated, his frown deepening. A gentle breeze ruffled the grass, cooling the sweat beginning to drip down

Karl's spine. The guard's nostrils flared as he took in the scents—he probably shifted into a scent-focused creature like a wolf—and he suddenly stiffened.

Lyric slowly climbed down from the wagon and sauntered past Karl on his way to Ralph's side. He rested an elbow on Ralph's shoulder, leaning indolently as he studied the guards.

Another breeze blew through the grass, passing over Lyric before wafting in the guard's faces. Nostrils flared again, and then as if their strings were cut, all the guards abruptly dropped to their knees, bowing their heads at an angle that exposed the backs of their necks.

"I have been sent on a diplomatic mission to speak with our neighbors in Toval about a pressing matter. These kind merchants have agreed to help me be discrete with my travels. Do you understand?" Lyric asked, his tone stern and authoritative, but not cold. "I commend you for the excellent work you are doing, following my dear uncle, the king's, orders. But I follow the king's orders as well, so I must ask you to move aside and allow us to pass."

"At once, Your Highness!" the lead guard forced out, his voice wobbling as if fear made it hard to get the words out. "Please cross at your leisure."

The guards awkwardly shuffled to the side without getting up or raising their heads. Ralph waved one hand, and Tilly guided the horses forward, onto the stone bridge. Karl followed along with everyone else on foot, trying his hardest to appear nonchalant, as if he escorted princes who shapeshifted into dragons every day. In reality, his heart was beating in his throat, and he kept having to remind himself to breathe.

The horses' hooves touched ground on the other side of the bridge, and then the front wheels of the wagon. The back wheels left the bridge and Karl quickly had to stiffen his knees to keep from collapsing in relief. Ama was safely back in Toval. Karl almost didn't notice when his own feet left the stone of the bridge, returning to the hard-packed brown dirt on the Toval side—he was too lightheaded—but he snapped back to reality as one of the Tovalian guards spoke.

"Welcome back, Lieutenant. Was your trip successful?"

"Mostly," Ralph replied with a scowl. "We're being pursued, and it's not the sort of problem that will honor international border regulations. We're moving out at top speed, and I'm ordering you to abandon your posts."

"Leave the border unguarded, sir?" another guard gasped out.

Ralph grimaced. "Unfortunately, yes. But if I know Commander Fen, I will bet you there's a contingent of the Royal Forces just out of sight. They'll help resecure the border after whatever is pursuing us gives up."

"Sir!" the first guard replied to Ralph with a salute. He turned to the other guards. "Wake the night shift and saddle all the horses. We're moving out with all haste!"

The faintest hint of dust from a large party approaching in the distance from Yaroi became visible as one of the guards brought a horse over for Karl to ride. The enemy was coming quickly, just as Lyric claimed, and they couldn't afford to get caught. Thankfully, within minutes, the guard house was empty, and they were back on the road, running from that growing plume of dust.

Hopefully Ralph was correct, and Fen was waiting for them only a few miles down the road. The border and one measly bridge wasn't going to stop their pursuers; their only chance of surviving this was if Fen had the Royal

Forces stationed nearby. That was the only way Ama was going to survive too.

Ama had to still be alive. He had to be. Karl couldn't check on him while they were moving, but he desperately wanted to. Even opening the secret hatch was too dangerous since Ama could roll out and fall to the ground. Instead, all Karl could do was ride nearby and hope Ama could somehow hear his desperate mental pleas to just hang on a little longer. If Fen had forces stationed nearby, he would have healers with him too. Ama only had to survive a little longer. *Just a little longer,* Karl repeated like a mantra as the road passed by beneath his horse's hooves.

The exhausted cart horses could only go so fast, but the same boring road quickly returned to the same monotony as before: brown dirt with wheel ruts cut into it with waving winter-brown grasses on either side. If Karl didn't have the sour memory full of worry and stress about getting across that bridge, he wouldn't know they had crossed into Toval.

A bird called from up ahead, which Karl found strange since their noisy group had scared any nearby animals into hiding. Ralph grinned, stood in his stirrups, and waved a hand over his head.

"It's us! Sprint back to camp and get Commander Fen. We've got company on our tail, about a half hour behind, and we've got wounded!" he yelled out.

A second later two soldiers appeared in the grass, already racing away. They didn't follow the path, cutting through the grass on a likely faster route. The road curved ahead, making their trajectory more obvious.

"They were the two-mile sentries," Ralph explained. "We're almost there."

Karl heard the camp before he saw them, the noise of a number of horses and humans in close proximity unmistakable in the otherwise empty plains. The road forked ahead, and Fen had set up camp right in the middle of that fork. Anyone passing through would need to go through them. The sentries had obviously passed along Ralph's message since everyone was bustling around. Soldiers were saddling horses and mounting in full armor to the left. To the right, the archers were warming their bows and getting crossbows set along with the spear and shield group preparing to repel oncoming riders. In the center stood their welcoming committee, and a more *welcome* sight Karl had never seen.

Fen was in the lead, Char standing right next to him. Fen had light brown hair and hazel eyes, and his body was muscled from years of military training and leading the Tovalian Royal Forces. Char had black hair and dark-blue eyes, and his smile today was the same one that had made Karl feel like he belonged that first day all those years ago when Fen had first dumped Karl on him. Behind Char was Uncle Caro's closest friend, Healer Alina, her gray-shot hair pulled into a tight braid, and her eyes anxious as she took them all in. Tilly stopped the wagon. Karl tumbled off his horse and dashed over to the compartment where Ama was concealed.

"Alina!" he yelled out, as he punched the hatch open. He got his hands underneath Ama's very still form, dragging his limp body out of the compartment by a grip on one arm and Ama's shirt in his other hand. Ama's head flopped, banging and scraping against the side of the compartment as Karl tried to carefully slide him free. Karl had to pause to get a better grip— his hands were shaking so much—but when he resumed pulling, other people arrived to help. Alina and Ralph together were able to lever Ama out and down to the ground. Karl dropped with them, his knees suddenly too weak to hold him up.

Ama looked dead. His skin was pale and lifeless, and his body motionless. Karl couldn't see any sign of his chest moving or that he was breathing at all.

"Damn," Alina swore as her hands began to glow green. She sank her magic into Ama, biting her lip as if it hurt.

"Is he—?" Karl cut himself off, unable to say the words out loud.

"Here," Ralph replied. He grabbed Karl's hand and placed it on Ama's neck. "Can you feel that?"

Faintly, like fluttering wings or Emily's stuttering footsteps when she was first learning to walk, the uneven beats of Ama's heart thumped weakly against Karl's pressing fingers. Ralph lifted his hand from Karl's, but Karl couldn't move just yet.

Alive. Not dead. Karl slumped, lightheaded as if he had been holding his breath too long. Maybe he had, Karl realized as he gasped for air.

"Ralph, I'm leaving you in charge of camp. Defenses should already be set up, but they may try to flank us, so be prepared," Fen was saying when Karl had the wherewithal to look up again. Fen was in full armor, holding the reins of his destrier, who also had armor on. Up ahead, Captain Zain, Emily's adoptive mother and one of the three captains under Fen's command, was glaring over at them, no doubt eager to be off already, a contingent of about fifty soldiers with her. She stood out in the crowd more for her sheer presence than her gorgeous dark skin and hair in thick braids. At least another fifty soldiers, most of them on foot with spear and bow at the ready, were waiting for Fen.

"Yes, Commander!" Ralph replied, saluting. Fen clapped him on the shoulder and strode off, and a moment later his forces were off with Captain Zain's in his wake.

Someone had helped Lady Ettine out of her hiding spot, and she stood off to the side with Lyric, watching Alina. Tilly was caring for the horses, who had worked far too hard the last few days and deserved a break. Emily…Karl sighed. Emily had vanished, which likely meant she was with Zain. She was obsessed with anything military, and Karl wouldn't be surprised if she ended up a commander at some point. Marc was busy pulling weapons out of that hidden compartment in the wagon. He strapped his own sword around his waist and brought over Ralph's as well.

"Here," Marc said to Karl as he placed two daggers onto the ground next to Karl. "I presume you're still as proficient with these as you were before you left?"

"I'm probably better now," Karl replied, able to joke thanks to the gentle thudding of Ama's heart against his fingertips. "The amount of meat I had to butcher with precision, and the fact that any errant knife cut a point off my final grade? I could slice you to ribbons before you even realized you were under attack."

"Hah. I'd like to see you try. Didn't you go to bakery school? What were you doing in a butchering class?" Marc asked, frowning at him.

"Not all pie and pastry fillings are sweet, you know. I aced the savory baking courses too."

Marc licked his lips. "Char makes the best shepherd's pie ever. I'd be happy to taste test yours sometime." He winked.

"Wouldn't we all," Ralph replied, standing. "For now, let's all get to our posts. I'm not dying because we were too lazy to watch our backs, not after everything it took to get us here in the first place."

Ralph strode off, Marc following, but Karl stayed where he was. Technically, he was a noncombatant, since he was officially hired by the

Royal Forces to work in the kitchen with Char. Unofficially, yes, joking aside, he really was very proficient with daggers in hand. He had always been, even as a kid, but after Char and Ralph had gotten kidnapped, and Karl had used his fighting abilities to help get them to safety, the Royal Forces had seen him properly and expertly trained. They had trained Shan and Emily too, but Shan was very happy to remain a sous chef and Emily…was off with Zain to fight in a real battle. Again. Telling Emily she was too young or just a kid had zero effect at deterring her; she instead snuck off as only a former street kid could and did whatever she wanted to do anyway. Karl didn't like it, but he had failed that fight with her too many times and at this point was resigned.

Alina suddenly let out a slow breath as she sat back on her heels. The green glow faded from her hands.

"How is he?" Karl asked. Ama's heartbeat felt a little steadier, although that could also be Karl projecting his hopes over reality.

"Stable, for now," she replied, rubbing her fingers over her eyebrows as if she was fighting off a headache. "One of the worst cases I've seen, to be honest. Luckily you had Emily to give him some strength, or I don't know that he would have made it." She looked up at Karl and gave him a small smile. "I put him in a medically induced coma to keep him from thrashing or waking up and trying to move. I need to give his body a chance to heal naturally for a bit before I use more magic on him. How about we get him into a bedroll by the fire? We can make him some honey tea."

Getting Ama off the ground and over to the fire in the center of camp took both of them, staggering along since Ama was definitely a deadweight. Char was already there when they arrived. He'd placed a steaming tin camping tea service onto the ground and opened the bedroll so they could slide Ama inside. Alina propped Ama up on her shoulder and took the teacup from Char, blowing on it until the steam faded before gently and slowly tipping it so the liquid dribbled into Ama's mouth. A moment later Ama swallowed and Alina dribbled more tea, repeating the process slowly, sip by sip, until the cup was empty. Karl helped Alina lay Ama down flat and covered him warmly with the bedroll.

Ama's breathing was slow and even. He was pale and waxy-looking, his lips dry and cracked and had black circles under his eyes, but he no longer looked dead.

"Let's leave him in peace while we can," Alina said, her voice soft and soothing as she gently placed a hand on Karl's shoulder to draw him away. "I think you and I could both also do with a cup of that tea, and I know someone has been anxiously waiting to say hello too."

She was right. Char's smile was immediate and still so welcoming as Alina left Karl at Char's side while she went to make more tea. Char opened his arms and Karl fell into the hug, relishing the warmth and comfort Char had never hesitated to give to the band of street waifs he had rescued.

"I won't say welcome home yet," Char said to the top of Karl's head, still squeezing him tight. "We've got a few more days travel before that. But I am glad you're back in Toval." He pulled away, but only to arm's length so he could look Karl up and down. "I think Alina's idea of some tea and food is a good one. You look like you've had a rough few days. Sit down and tell me all about your time at Timmonsville while I make you something."

This really was almost like being home. Char fussing and cooking, always serene, so long as he had some sort of food to prepare, even while surrounded by military-style chaos. Karl sat on the ground near where Char was busy stirring something that bubbled in a massive cauldron hanging in a tripod over the fire. He was content to wait for the Royal Forces to return from battle and talk with his adoptive father as if he had nothing else to worry about in life.

Chapter Eleven

THE RESPITE WAS short-lived. Karl was only halfway through drinking a cup of sweet honey tea interspersed with bites of herb-buttered toast—Karl had zero idea how Char had managed to keep butter fresh out here, and he wasn't about to ask—when the first sounds of battle began to echo over the plains. The shouts of fighters and metallic crash of swords and shields were unmistakable, even from a distance.

Char let out a slow breath, grimacing into his tea, and Alina sighed, but they both looked resigned. Lyric and Melody sat together on the other side of the fire with their own tea and toast, and neither looked particularly worried. Karl tried to emulate all of them, taking another sip of tea with feigned nonchalance. He had lived in the Royal Forces barracks for years and had heard plenty of stories about battles and brilliant strategies winning the day, but aside from a handful of street fights, he had never actually been near a real battle.

Char stood and went to stir his cauldron, still grimacing. He didn't always deploy with the troops, Karl knew, but he also knew Char was much more used to waiting for a battle to end while the fighting raged around him than Karl would ever be. Knowing Fen was out in whatever mess they were only residually hearing had to be hell for Char, and yet all he was doing was stirring the stew he had cooked for their postbattle meal.

"I trust him, and them," Char suddenly said, looking at Karl. "I trust the training and preparation they go through every day, and I believe in Fen's promise that he'll see me later." He shook his head. "Since I know they'll be hungry when they return, this is what I can do for them in support."

Char retook his seat and returned to his tea. Alina patted his arm and opened her mouth to say something when a new round of yelling and arms clashing started up, this time much closer. A howl sounded, followed by a man's scream.

"They must have flanked Fen," Ralph called as he and three others dashed through the camp, past the fire on their way toward the noise. "Stay here!"

Ralph was excellent at his job, the best swordsman in the Royal Forces. When Captain Wong had retired last year and Fen's previous second in command, Jensen, was promoted, Ralph had turned down his own promotion to Fen's second. In a letter sent while he was away in training, Char had told him Ralph preferred field work and being Char's bodyguard. Still, no matter how amazing Ralph might be, he only had three men at his back.

Decided, Karl stood and drew his daggers before jogging after Ralph. He glanced back when he heard footsteps following to see Char holding a dagger, his hands and arms glowing blue, and Lyric jogging next to him, grinning.

Two soldiers lay on the ground, not moving. Ralph and his group had formed a diamond with their backs facing one another, all of them fighting about ten wolves and two men on horseback. Karl's group hit the wolves' flank. He cut at the closest wolf, slicing through fur into muscle, and the wolf went down with a pained yelp and spray of blood. Alerted, the wolves spun and one of the men on horseback headed their way.

Lyric picked up one of the swords the dropped fighters had left behind and started swinging. Char was a master at using his magic to deflect blades—he used it primarily to prevent cutting himself in the kitchen, but Karl had seen how effective it was in battle before. However, Char wasn't the only one who knew how to add magic to his fighting. Karl concentrated as he swung a knife to block swiped claws and a faint red sheen appeared along his blade. Blood didn't flow when his knife met flesh, but the agonized scream as the wolf suddenly shifted into human and curled around the festering, puss-filled wound on his thigh was just as effective.

A lynx suddenly pounced on the wolf in front of Karl, taking it down and ripping out its throat. Emily dashed past, her short sword bloody, but Karl couldn't focus on them as another wolf ran at him.

He sliced and jabbed, spinning to try to keep the enemy in front. Using daggers meant he had to get close to engage, but he was fast and accurate, and one slice from his magic incapacitated his enemy.

Karl's arms were burning, and he was panting for breath when he turned again to find another enemy to fight and only found allies still standing. He slowly dropped his hands to his sides, gasping, and his muscles started to shake from the exertion he had just put them through.

"Report!" Ralph yelled from somewhere to Karl's left. He looked in that direction and found Ralph and Marc standing back-to-back, both scanning the area. Emily scurried over, followed by Tilly and the three guards in Ralph's original group. Karl's breathing was finally slowing, but he didn't let out a full breath until Char and Lyric also walked into view, the lynx pacing at Lyric's feet. Karl hurried over to join them, and a moment later, Alina ran into the battlefield. She fell on the two fallen guardsmen, her hands glowing green.

"Casualties?" Ralph was saying to one of the guards Karl didn't know when Karl reached him.

"Just the two sentries from this side of camp. Healer Alina is working on them now," the guard replied.

Ralph nodded sharply. "Right. You two, I want you to complete a full patrol around the camp. Make sure the rest of our sentries are not in any trouble. You two"—he turned to Tilly and the third guard Karl didn't know—"triage the enemy. I want bodies searched and moved to somewhere we can bury them, and anyone injured should be bandaged until the healers with Commander Fen return. Keep in mind the wolves will likely shapeshift into human form."

All four saluted and ran off.

Ralph next turned to Lyric and the lynx sitting at his feet. "Your Highnesses," he said, bowing shallowly. "Thank you for aiding us in this battle. Please go take some time to rest, and I will do my best to ensure the rest of your journey is uneventful."

"A bit of invigorating battle helped fight off the travel doldrums," Lyric replied with what Karl was starting to believe was the smile he kept on his face to mask whatever he was actually thinking. "We'll go wash off the blood though."

He nodded to Ralph, and then Lyric and Melody headed back into camp.

Ralph sighed and shook his head but apparently let it go. Instead, he lifted a hand and lightly bonked Emily on the top of her head with a loose fist. "You know you're not supposed to join in any battles yet, not until you're old enough to actually enlist."

"It's special circumstances," Emily replied, frowning grumpily as she purposefully glanced around at the remnants of their battlefield.

"You think Captain Zain would accept that as an excuse?" Ralph answered, frowning back at her. After a moment, he sighed again and rolled his eyes. "Fine. She'll figure it out even if you don't tell her, so when she corners you about it, tell her I've already tripled both your training time and your time on cleaning duty when we get back to the barracks."

"Aww." Emily kicked at the ground, but didn't argue beyond that one groan.

"Go get cleaned up, and then you're helping Char prep dinner," Ralph finished, shooing her away in the direction of camp. Emily obeyed, slouching off, but thankfully not whining any more.

The soldiers Ralph sent on patrol jogged back, saluting Ralph.

"Karl, you go get cleaned up too. I'm sure Ama could use more tea by now as well." Ralph turned to get the report from his soldiers, but he was right. There wasn't anything more Karl could do here.

Melody was sitting next to Char by the fire when Karl returned to his abandoned toast and tea. He had cleaned his blades and changed into a fresh shirt first but was glad to see Char already had fresh tea waiting.

"This one's lukewarm," Char explained as he passed Karl one of the travel cups. "No one bothered him while you were gone."

"Thanks." Karl took the cup over to the other side of the fire where Ama lay, still asleep in his bedroll. After a bit of maneuvering, Karl was able to lever Ama up, his body resting against Karl's chest, so Karl had one hand to steady Ama's head and the other to gently tip tea into his mouth. He was careful to only give Ama a sip at a time, and Ama swallowed as if he was thirsty, but he didn't open his eyes or otherwise indicate he noticed Karl was with him. Still, Ama's breathing was even and his skin was cool. The black circles under his eyes were pronounced, but no worse than before.

Once the cup was empty, Karl slid Ama back into the bedroll as gently as possible, making sure he was completely covered before leaving him in peace to let Alina's magic keep working on him.

Emily had joined Char and Melody by the fire while Karl was distracted. She had finally changed out of her little girl costume, the pigtails and pretty clothes gone, replaced by the working leathers most of the Royal Forces wore when they were out on an assignment where they didn't need armor. No one was going to make armor for a growing girl—just the leathers were expensive enough—but she looked like a completely different person. Melody kept glancing over at where Emily was grumpily chopping something for Char as if she couldn't believe what her eyes were telling her.

Thankfully, before Karl had to figure out something to say to break the ice, Fen and Zain, and all the soldiers who had been fighting the Yaroi incursion, returned. The camp roared as it filled, humans and horses taking up all the empty places. Loud, boisterous people letting off steam and anxiety, healers and hostlers running back and forth—the din was deafening yet comforting at the same time.

Char's lips lifted in the slightest smile as Fen strode through camp, calling out orders as he passed different groups until he reached Char's side. Char smiled and sank into the arm Fen wrapped over his shoulders, his head resting on Fen's shoulder.

"Now all that's left for this journey is returning home to Etoval," Char said, looking over at Karl, his smile growing. "We'll be home soon."

Interlude

AMA DIDN'T KNOW where he was, what day it was, or even why he was in a quiet room where everything around him was white. The last thing he remembered was that cramped compartment, getting jostled and bruised every time the wagon went over a bump, and feeling like the world was starting to spin around him. Now he was lying in a soft bed with thick blankets, in a small room with a tall cabinet as the only other furniture. The walls, blankets, and cabinet were all stark white. The only color in the room was the silver of the doorknob across the room from the bed.

There was no way anyone from Yaroi would put him up in such luxury. Even bland-white luxury was still better than the cell and quick execution waiting for him should he ever set foot in Yaroi again. Which meant he had to be either in Namin or Toval, most likely Toval, since that was the direction they had been heading last he remembered. Of course, he had no idea how long ago that had been nor whether something had happened to derail their journey. For all he knew, they could be in the secretive enclave that was the country of Zafindere, a country high in the mountains.

Ama really hoped they weren't there, and though the chances of that were low, the mystery of where he was continued to churn through his mind. He wanted to get up and go find someone to fill him in on everything he'd missed, but when he shifted position to move the blankets out of the way, a lock of his very blond hair slipped down into view.

He had decided— No, he had *sworn* to himself. Hanging on that whipping cross, enduring the sharp agony of each magic-enhanced slice of the whip across his back, he had promised that if he was able to escape he was done pretending. Ama would finally tell the truth about himself to the people who mattered to him. He'd wanted to tell Braxton everything, but then Karl had appeared and telling Karl everything now felt more important than ever.

Karl had an innocent demeanor, but he hid a life and a mind that was anything *but* innocent behind his facade. His eyes were such an amazing shade of golden brown, as if the golden shade of royal magic had mixed with something to become so much stronger. Hidden in those eyes was the same knowledge of the darker side of the world Ama had, based on things they had both experienced as children that led them onto the paths they had chosen. Ama became Braxton's spy. Karl became Fen's.

But… Ama let out a sigh, sliding that lock of hair between two fingers before resolutely tucking it back behind one ear. His life as a spy was now over. Thanks to the debacle in Yaroi, Yaroi knew all about Ama the spy. Every shadow he tried to slip into to continue his work would have a Yarokian assassin waiting for him. Ama the spy therefore had to vanish forever, replaced with a new identity. Or, in Ama's case, an old identity he had hidden away a long time ago.

As Ama had told Karl back in the woods when he washed the dye out of his hair, for the first time others could see he was both a prince of Namin and Toval, nephew to Queen Carmillian through his mother and to King Aurelius through his father. His magic proved that connection. He could only see the present and always knew when danger was lurking ahead. That had helped him greatly as a spy and proved his connection to the Namese throne. The Tovalian royal power was the ability to summon weapons. Fen and Braxton could pull swords out of nothingness; Ama could summon a small dagger. His power was diluted, the perfect example of why royal families did not intermarry their children born with the royal power.

Ama could continue to hide his power, but assuming his birth identity meant he could not hide his features any longer. His golden-colored hair proved his Namese heritage, distinctive to the royal family thanks to their golden magic staining their features, and his face looked too much like his father's. Anyone who remembered what traitor Prince Randolph looked like would easily recognize Ama.

All of which boiled down to the fact that he needed to know where he was and who was with him before he started wandering around looking for answers. He needed to be patient and wait for someone to come to him, after which he would hopefully know what was going on.

Ama fell into a light doze as he waited. Since he didn't have a clock, and the light through the window was heavily filtered by the blinds, he had no idea how much time passed. When someone knocked lightly on the door, he jolted awake.

Whoever knocked didn't bother waiting for him to call out, letting themselves in while he was still blearily blinking sleep out of his eyes. Two people walked in, the second gently shutting the door behind her.

"Karl," Ama said, breathing out in relief as Karl smiled at him, as bright and happy as Ama remembered. "Does this mean we made it to Etoval?" The woman behind him was older, but she also looked vaguely familiar, which meant she had probably been part of the coup in Namin somehow.

Karl nodded. "We crossed the border two weeks ago and made it to Etoval last week. Alina here had to put you in a magically induced coma to help you recover, but she said you're well enough to leave the healing ward now."

"As long as you don't do anything to overexert yourself," Alina added, wagging her finger firmly at him. "It took a lot for me to put you back together. I won't be happy if you end up right back here because you do too much too soon!"

"I suspect I won't be allowed to do anything much," Ama replied, pointedly tugging at a lock of his hair.

"They announced your return to Etoval two days ago, when Alina decided it would be safe to slowly wake you," Karl explained. "You had been hidden away to protect you from your father and because of your connection to the future queen of Namin, but now that her rule is secure, you've decided to return to court again. We're pretending you were here as a baby, and no one remembers because the royal family went to great lengths to erase you to keep you safe," Karl added with a rueful grin. "You should expect some indelicate questions about what it was like living in a tiny farming village, but we figured keeping the rest of your story as close to the truth as possible would be easiest for you."

"I see," Ama replied. Any chance of his influencing the decision to announce him was gone, but in the end what Karl had explained was probably the best option. Ama suspected Aunt Millie's involvement.

"Queen Carmillian told us your real name, by the way," Karl added, rubbing the back of his neck as he confirmed Ama's suspicions. "She was worried Yaroi might know you by Ama, but she said they won't know Casmir. Uncle Braxton said you would hate it, but you would also understand you didn't really have a choice."

Ama—no, he was Casmir now, exactly as he had promised himself he would be—Casmir sighed. "He was right. I hate it, but I see the utility. I guess I should just be glad they were so willing to accept me, considering who my father was."

"They took me in too," Karl replied with an easy shrug. "I'm a nobody off the street, yet they willingly adopted me into their family. They even sent me to escort you around the palace as proof that you had full royal support."

"On that note," Alina said, cutting in, "it's time for you to take Casmir to his new room."

Karl nodded. "Yeah, that's why I'm here. I'm supposed to show you the way to the royal wing and your new room, and then, it you're feeling up to it, bring you to afternoon tea and then dinner."

"Here are your clothes," Alina added, holding out a cloth-wrapped package Casmir hadn't noticed she was holding. "We'll wait outside while you get changed."

Casmir took the clothes from her and waited for Karl and Alina to leave before he started changing. Too much had happened in the last five minutes and Casmir didn't know which thought to dwell on first. Maybe the fact that he had slipped so easily into mentally calling himself Casmir. Ever since the day Randolph had returned to their village and Casmir had needed to go into hiding as Ama, no one had called him that. He had been Ama for so long that sliding into becoming Casmir should have been difficult, yet here he was, accepting it so easily.

Maybe it was his promise to be his real self, or maybe the fact that he had apparently spent two weeks in a coma. Or, maybe it was Karl's awkward yet understanding smile when he had called him Casmir for the first time. Somehow Karl's presence made everything feel easier for Casmir.

The pants were blue but embroidered at the pockets with yellow flowers. The shirt was white, but the jacket was also blue with yellow flowers. It all fit well enough Casmir wondered if someone had come to measure him in his sleep. Soft, brown ankle boots completed the outfit.

He pulled open the door and stepped into a wide room in the shape of an octagon. Two rows of beds filled the center of the room. Doors and cabinets covered the walls. Karl and Alina were waiting beside a pair of open double doors on the far side of the room. Casmir joined them. They said goodbye to Alina, and Casmir followed Karl into the rest of the castle.

They walked side by side through the hallways, Karl pointing out landmarks and anything interesting as they went. Casmir didn't have the heart to tell Karl he had been here many times before, concealed in the uniforms of various employees as he snuck around to report to Braxton. Being here as himself, without having to hide, was strange though. Casmir suspected he would feel like that for a long, long time.

The healer's wing was on the other side of the palace from the royal wing. They walked for a long time. At first, Casmir focused on trying to dispel the strangeness and then he moved on to simply enjoying this chance to spend some time with Karl.

Something about Karl drew Casmir in. Yes, Karl had saved Casmir from certain death, and yes, there were some wonderful hidden depths to Karl that intrigued Casmir, but what drew him was something more—Karl's smile, shy yet knowing and Karl's swagger that said he had some sort of high-level weapons training, though he had literally just finished school to be a baker. He was a dichotomy of opposites, and Casmir wanted to know more. He wanted to know everything about Karl, and… Casmir swallowed hard, remembering the way he'd started to feel from the first time back at the pond in Yaroi, when Karl had helped him bathe and wash his hair, wanting to invite Karl closer and wanting to open up to tell Karl all about himself. Casmir craved giving Karl everything he wished Karl might one day give him.

He forced those thoughts aside, shoving them to the back of his mind. Now wasn't the time to be distracted. He was the mystery prince once hidden away and now returned to claim his birthright. The rest of the castle and the court must be ravenously curious, and Casmir wouldn't be surprised to learn someone planned to take revenge on him for the terrible things his father had done. He needed to pay careful attention to his surroundings and not be distracted by impossible wishes.

The people they passed along their route stared, their gazes fixed on him and Karl, then turning their heads to watch as they walked by. And yet…

Casmir frowned internally, keeping his outward expression full of bland interest as Karl pointed out a lovely mosaic of white button flowers twined around musical instruments inlaid into the floor as they walked across an atrium and into yet another hallway. There were definitely plenty of people looking at Casmir. He could feel their eyes burning into his back. And yet…

When Casmir and Karl walked into an occupied space, the person who caught most of the attention of the gawkers wasn't Casmir. No, the nobles and courtiers, lawyers and secretaries, and even the servants were all focused on Karl instead.

Karl was certainly an interesting individual, beyond even Casmir's infatuation. He was a former thief turned baker working for the Royal Forces who had been adopted by Char, husband of Prince Fen. Karl was practically a prince by adoption, even though Fen hadn't been able to make it official. However, nothing about Karl's history was new to the court and certainly shouldn't eclipse the return of a prince from exile, particularly when that prince was the son of the greatest traitor in Tovalian history. Something was clearly going on, and Casmir had a strange feeling whatever it was wouldn't end well for Karl.

Casmir let out a slow breath as they reached the guards stationed outside the royal wing. He said some pleasantries when Karl introduced him, but behind that outward mask, his brain was churning. Casmir might not be able to fade back into the shadows again, as his life as a spy was over, but that didn't mean his abilities needed to go to waste. He was going to find out what was going on with Karl and use every trick in his repertoire to ensure Karl survived.

No matter what the cost.

Chapter Twelve

"WE WENT BACK eight generations," Braxton said, lounging back in his chair on the other side of his desk. His public office was a mess of papers and books absolutely everywhere, stacked on every flat surface and all over the floor, turning the path to the visitor's chair where Karl sat in into a dangerous maze.

"You couldn't find anyone?" Karl asked, his heart sinking.

"It's not that we couldn't find anyone willing," Braxton replied with a sneer and disappointed shake of his head. "Plenty of people were all too happy with the idea of getting their hands on the wealth from the Bay of Whist. All those tax dollars coming in at that port would let anyone live a comfortable life of excess. The previous Baron Whistfield certainly did when he was turning traitor to the crown."

"There has to be one person you can choose as heir who wouldn't be too bad, right?"

Braxton sighed, shaking his head again. "I'm sure somewhere in those eight generations there was one. The problem isn't needing a blood heir like royal law dictates. The Whistfield inheritance has its own mandate on top of the royal one. It states the heir must be someone who wields red magic, to the point that a non-blood heir with the magic would inherit over a blood heir without."

Braxton slumped in his seat and ran a hand through his hair, giving Karl a look Karl really wished he couldn't interpret.

"No one in those eight generations had the magic, did they?" Karl asked, even though Braxton's expression had already told him it was a redundant question. Karl didn't bother waiting for Braxton to answer, instead stating the answer himself. "No one, that is, except me."

Braxton nodded. "We couldn't find anyone else of the bloodline with red magic, neither in those eight generations nor by searching for other bastard children like you. Royal law dictates if a blood heir can be located, we are mandated to declare them the heir. You are the heir to the Barony of Whistfield, and unlike four years ago, this time you can't turn it down."

"Damn," Karl breathed out, joining Braxton in slumping down in his seat. "I don't want anything to do with a noble title."

Whistfield might only be a barony, but because of Toval's largest port being located in the Bay of Whist, it had the money and resources to rival a duke at times. Karl had turned down the crown's offer four years ago, when the baron at the time—Karl's father—had committed treason and been executed. The baron's only legitimate child and his younger brother had both died in the fighting, leaving only Karl as the bastard child with the ability to use red magic.

"Explains why I've been feeling murderous gazes tracking me

whenever I'm walking in any of the public hallways. Bet all those younger sons or weaker nobles want nothing more than to take their fancy, bejeweled daggers and plunge what's probably dull metal into my back."

Braxton snorted out a laugh. "Graphic, but probably accurate. Do us all a favor and stay with Casmir when you're wandering around the castle. He might be settling pretty well into the role of innocent prince, but he's still deadly. If any of those dull blades head your way, he'll have your back."

"You realize I'm armed right now too?" Karl grumped out, trying to conceal the way his heart leapt at the idea of getting to spend time with Casmir. "Why couldn't I have gone with Char and Fen on the Royal Forces annual training? You know, wherever they went…" Which was somewhere out in the wild, unsettled areas of Toval where they could train intensely for three to four weeks uninterrupted. The barracks in the military complex were empty. Even Emily had gone with them, leaving Karl and Shan behind.

Sous chefs were always in high demand, so Shan had settled without trouble into the castle's kitchens with Terrance, Char's cousin. Bakers, on the other hand… Not so much. Karl sighed. Terrance had offered to find Karl space, but Karl knew the only way Terrance could do that was to kick someone else out. Karl wasn't about to cost someone their job just so he could fill some empty hours in his day, or so he could escape bloodthirsty courtiers.

"They went somewhere, but you know you would just be in the way there. They can't help you train with your knives while they're busy with their own maneuvers, and they don't need a baker." Braxton shrugged. "You're needed here anyway, as the Baron Whistfield." He reached into one of the stacks of papers and pulled out a section as thick as his fist. "Here's an overview of your lands and responsibilities, some paperwork you have to fill out to get everything transferred into your name, including bank forms and some stuff for the lawyers, and a few other things like arranging for the jeweler to help you design your signet ring." He passed the papers over to Karl. "I'll need everything you have to review and sign back by tomorrow, so I can get it all to Ayer and get the ball moving on your debut in court as the new baron."

"A debut? Why do we need that? Just slap the title on me. In a few weeks the Royal Forces will be back, and I'll return to their kitchen to bake every day. The second a new scandal hits, I'll be yesterday's news and completely forgotten. All of this will blow over soon enough."

Karl hoped the fleeting look of pity that crossed and then disappeared from Braxton's face didn't mean what the heavy feeling in his stomach coupled by the weight of the papers in his hands implied.

"Focus on getting through all that paperwork first," Braxton replied. "Then we can figure out your baking."

Karl bit his lip but nodded. He stood to leave but paused with his hand on his chair back to turn toward Braxton.

"Have you heard anything from Yaroi?" he asked.

In the weeks since Karl had been back in Etoval, he had spent the early mornings baking the day's breads and pies for the Royal Forces, before heading to the castle to help nurse Casmir back to health. Once Casmir had left the healer's wing two weeks ago, Karl had been able to focus a lot of his time on preparing the foodstuffs for the Royal Forces' expedition. Now that the Royal Forces were gone and Karl was staying in Fen's set of rooms in the royal wing, he had far too much time for his thoughts to drift and to dwell on that terrible journey out of Yari.

Braxton frowned, pursing his lips in thought before he replied, "No, and we should have. They definitely know we have two members of their royal household here in Etoval, but we haven't received any sort of diplomatic communications. Not even their ambassador stationed here has spoken to us about it."

"And it's Yaroi, so if they're not willing to be open about it—"

"It means they're doing something underhanded. Yes," Braxton finished. "I've kept alert, but I've yet to uncover anything."

That was likely all Braxton could say aloud since they were in his public office. His private one was much more secure and also hidden. Karl had only been there twice. Thankfully, Karl could read between the lines. Braxton had tasked his spies, had investigated, and then done whatever else a spymaster could do to obtain information, and had come up with nothing.

"I'll keep a lookout too, and will let you know if I spot anything," Karl said.

"I appreciate it," Braxton replied, smiling at him. "Now go deal with that paperwork."

Karl grimaced, glaring down at the mass of papers he needed two hands to hold properly. Somehow, from the moment he had stepped off the boat in Yari, all his plans for where he wanted to go in life were slowly getting derailed one by one. He walked into the hallway, closed the door behind him, and headed off in the general direction of the royal wing. The castle was busy as usual, servants and courtiers everywhere, and since these days everyone noticed him, Karl had to deal with their angry and envious stares as he made his way.

As Karl walked past one of the many entrances to the expansive gardens, Casmir's voice made him pause. He turned to look out into the garden flush with buds just starting to open and show their vibrant blooms as spring finally began to take hold. Casmir was too far away to hear what he was actually saying, and outwardly he had a genial expression on his face, but something about the tilt to his lips and the sharpness in his eyes said he was annoyed and barely holding on to his temper.

"Cas!" Karl called out, waving over his head with one hand while hoping he was embarking on a rescue rather than getting in Casmir's way. "Are you heading back now? I'll walk with you."

Casmir's eyes softened as he waved back. He nodded politely to the group before walking over.

"Busy morning?" he asked Karl, eying Karl's morass of papers.

"I don't want to talk about it," Karl grumbled, pouting. Still, he sorted through his stack until he found the most damning piece of paper in the lot, then passed it over for Casmir to read. "It looks like your morning isn't going much better though."

"I'm just dealing with morons who think the fancy private education their parents paid for equates to real life experience," Casmir responded, frowning as he read. One eyebrow lifted when he got to the line that made Karl grit his teeth.

The title, lands, and honors of the Barony of Whistfield are hereby and henceforth bestowed upon the rightful blooded heir, Lord Karlow Musen Whist, the Baron Whistfield. Karl's stomach clenched just reading the words over Casmir's shoulder.

"Your inheriting this is definitely good for Toval, you know. When you called out to me just now, I was attending a tea with a number of nobles' sons and daughters, some of them heirs. I just had an absolutely riveting discussion about how to properly punish their servants because they served strawberry pie rather than the apple the noble brat demanded." Sarcasm clung to every word Casmir said, like slime on a frog.

"It's spring right now?" Karl asked, glancing out a nearby window that showed the same early buds on the trees outside. "Strawberries are in season. A bag of dried apple slices likely costs good gold this time of year. The cost of fresh apples to make a proper pie would be astronomical."

"Hmm, yes," Casmir replied, handing the paper back to Karl. "But they wanted apple; therefore, their servants needed to suffer. Horrendous."

"If I were their parents, I would have rewarded those servants for not wasting good gold on such a frivolous request."

Casmir laughed, his eyes bright with mirth as he looked at Karl. "You assume the apple didn't fall from the same tree. Besides, any of the useful nobles who actually contribute to this kingdom are far too busy this time of day with actual work. You'll be another noble doing work rather than playing, which will definitely help Toval. Only the useless fops fritter away their daytime hours on impractical tea parties."

The way Casmir's eyes glinted and the upward tilt to one side of his mouth was all Karl needed to read between the lines. Braxton had asked Casmir to befriend some of the fops, to be taken into their confidence and hopefully derail any foolishness they might start before it could escalate. Or, perhaps Casmir had taken on the task himself, knowing it would help Braxton. He might be a prince now, but he could still contribute as a spy too.

Casmir looked good. His hair was pulled back into a neat tail, showing off the emerald studs in his ears—newly pierced, Karl believed—which matched the deep green of his jacket and pants. Every inch of him looked like a prince. Part of this was Casmir's acting ability, honed by his years as a spy, but the role of prince seemed to fit him, as if he had shed an outer shell to reveal his true self underneath. Compared to Casmir, Karl definitely didn't look the part of a baron. He was wearing the usual brown pants allotted to any of the Royal Forces members for when they were off duty. As a concession to being in the palace, Karl had worn a blue shirt instead of the standard white, but the cut was the same simple and utilitarian one. He didn't wear any jewelry, nor did he have the presence to stand tall and look the part. No, Karl looked exactly like what he was: a street waif turned kitchen servant carrying a fat stack of papers like he was hoping the words wouldn't explode and try to eat him.

They finally reached the guards outside the royal wing and spent a few minutes saying hello, before heading for their rooms.

"What are you doing the rest of today?" Casmir asked as Karl stopped outside the door leading into Fen's private set of rooms.

"Probably going through this paperwork and wishing I was anyone else's bastard child. What about you?"

Casmir laughed. "Don't we all wish that. You mind if I keep you company while you bitch over whatever additional nonsense is in those papers? I'll call for tea."

"You're always welcome," Karl replied easily, opening the door and waving for Casmir to precede him, hoping his joy at knowing Casmir wanted to spend more time with Karl wasn't too obvious.

"Lovely. You can listen to me bitch about the other moronic things I had to listen to all morning, when you need a distraction," Casmir added as he led the way inside and headed for the bellpull to call a servant for tea.

Karl settled on one of the couches and dumped his papers onto the coffee table there. Casmir finished speaking with the servant who had appeared at the door and sat across from Karl.

"Right then," Karl began. He picked the first piece of paper off the stack and, with a grimace, got to work.

Chapter Thirteen

KARL LEFT THE papers on the table in the sitting area when he went to bed that night, but despite closing his eyes and trying to breathe slowly, sleep didn't come. He groaned and rolled over, rubbing his fingers on his forehead. With the curtains over the four-poster bed drawn, as well as the curtains over the window, he couldn't tell what time it was. The castle was rarely quiet and dark. Parties went all night and the business of running a kingdom didn't stop just because the sun had set. Shan was still in the kitchens, working the late shift to fulfill orders for whatever might come up this late. Still, the royal wing was as far from the bustle as it was possible to get and it was certainly quieter than the constant din of the military complex. Karl ought to be able to go to sleep.

Every time he closed his eyes the words on those damned papers floated into view, taunting him. Signing and sending off the handful of documents that confirmed his new status as Baron Whistfield was easy, almost anticlimactic, and yet the reality of it weighed on him.

Baron. From a homeless thief to one of the richest and most powerful men in the kingdom, and all it took was some ink on a piece of paper to make that a reality. He was a baker who sometimes did little extra jobs for Braxton on the side. The idea of court was terrifying. Karl had no idea how Casmir had acclimated so well, even if his acclimatization was part of whatever game he was currently playing as prince on Braxton's behalf.

Karl rolled over again, smushing his face into his pillow. He closed his eyes, willing, begging, for sleep to come. Time passed—he didn't know how much, only that he lay there unmoving and completely awake.

Finally, Karl rolled over yet again and let out a sigh as he gave up. He clearly wasn't going to sleep tonight, and he didn't see any point in torturing himself by trying.

Karl pushed the bed curtains out of the way as he sat up and moved to the edge of the bed. There wasn't really any point in getting up either. If he went out into the castle, he would be the center of everyone's immediate attention. Their stares would be even worse than normal, too, because despite the fact it that had only been a few hours and completed quietly, the entire castle would know he was officially the baron anyway. He would be judged for everything from his clothing choices to the way he walked, and that would affect his future life here far more than being judged as Fen's sort of adoptive son had ever been.

Which meant he needed to leave the castle and go into the city if he wanted any peace.

Sneaking out wasn't ideal, but this wouldn't be the first time Karl had spent the night wandering. His thieving days might be over, but the Royal Forces had trained him to expand those skills. Sometimes his going out to the city at night was for fun; sometimes the Royal Forces or Braxton had a mission for him. Tonight, he would be running from them all, and it would be worth it.

Karl hopped down from the bed and went to the wardrobe to dig out some going-out clothes. Nondescript pants and a shirt that wouldn't stand out as too fancy were part of his standard city clothes and were easy to pull on, so it wasn't long before Karl crept out into the hallway. He zipped along the lush carpet, not meeting anyone until he reached the guards stationed at the servant's entrance in the royal wing. On the other side of the door the stairs and dumbwaiter were tucked away, allowing for a direct line to the kitchens a few stories below. A couple other doors along the stairs also led to the laundry and other useful locations.

Karl waved to the guards as he went past and hopped down the stairs two at a time until he slipped into one of the sewing rooms a few flights down. The laundry was busy day and night, which actually made it easier to become part of the bustle and sneak into the raised courtyard where all the drying lines were filled with clean laundry. Down two more flights of stairs and he was in the rear garden. From there, he wended his way out to the wall and a back gate. One of the four guards manning the gate grinned at him, but they let him out without a fight or any questions. Braxton's standing orders to let him run around as he wanted must still be in effect even though Karl had been away for two years at school.

The gate was primarily used by servants who lived in the city but worked in the castle, so it led directly into the servant's warren of narrow paths that wound through most of the wealthier portions of the city. Even after two years away, Karl knew the paths like the back of his hand. As he set out, he didn't have a destination in mind and thought that he would wander aimlessly to see if anything had changed, but his feet apparently had other ideas.

The previous Baron Whistfield had revealed his part in the coup scheme when he had ordered Char be kidnapped and was arrogant enough to bring Char to the dungeon beneath his own house. Karl had helped Char escape and had been able to point his finger right at the house when the Royal Forces wanted to have words with the owner. The gate into the neglected garden behind the house where Karl's feet eventually stopped was therefore familiar. He stared at the gate for a long moment before finally forcing himself to look past it to the house beyond. He owned a house. Karl, the street urchin turned kitchen junkie, was rich enough to own his own house—and this was just the smallest bit of everything he now had—thanks to a little ink on paper. His life had clearly gone completely topsy-turvy, but he didn't have to completely abandon who he was. Like his neglected house, Karl simply had to find a way to rebuild and incorporate his old self with the new in a way that didn't force him to lose what was important to him in the process.

The manor's back garden was entirely overgrown, the scraggly lawn now a burgeoning forest choked with weeds and creeper vine. The building itself didn't look too bad after four years of abandonment, but there was no telling what the inside looked like. The Royal Forces had likely ransacked the place during their search for evidence or for any clues about the coup, and that mess was very likely still untouched. The first thing Karl needed to do with his newfound wealth was to hire people to fix the house here, as well as secretaries and accountants to figure out what was going on with his actual estate on the coast. The task was daunting, but he couldn't back away from any of it. Braxton had been very clear about his responsibilities.

However, Karl could also imagine a few ways he could continue his clandestine work for Braxton by hiding behind the title and money, similar to what he was pretty certain Casmir was doing. Being the Baron therefore wouldn't be all bad. He hoped.

Karl let out a heavy breath, snorting air through his nose as he took one last look at the back of the house. Since he was here, he ought to at least peek in some windows to see how bad the damage was. He couldn't get inside through the overgrown garden though. Instead, Karl returned to the servant's paths, heading for the junction with a path leading to the main road.

This early in the morning, the paved main road was even more deserted than the servant's paths. Karl didn't see a single person as he walked back toward the house. Except, as he turned a corner, an older woman sat on the front step of the building there. Her hair was completely gray and her face deeply creased with wrinkles. Karl estimated she was in her mid-to-late-seventies. What slowed his steps was the way she sat, her back braced against the closed door behind her and her head tipped back to look up into the eaves as if the answer to all her problems might be hidden underneath the tiled roof.

"Is everything okay?" Karl whispered, aware of the houses nearby where people were actually asleep.

She slowly lowered her head to look at him. Her eyes narrowed into a glare and her lips thinned into a scowl.

"I'm not selling, and that's final! You can dig the deed out from my decaying bones after I'm dead!"

Karl gaped for a moment, completely at a loss. "Umm," he stuttered out, unable to come up with something more intelligent.

"Only person who's going to get their hands on this property is someone who knows what they're doing in a damned bakery. Not someone who only wants the property because of the location!" she continued her rant, finally providing a bit of context to help ground Karl.

"This is a bakery?" he asked, glancing around. There was no sign over the door and the windows were firmly shuttered, but the chimney visible through the roof was larger than needed for just a house.

"Best dammed bakery in the entire city," she said, preening a bit as some of the suspicion faded from her glare. "At least, it was." She held out her hands, showing him the thickened knuckles that said arthritis had ended her days of kneading dough and beating egg whites.

Karl closed his mouth and smiled at her. "I don't get to this part of town all that often. I had no idea there was a bakery here. What sort of baked goods do you specialize in?"

Her glare faded a bit more. "Over there's the hoity-toity part of town," she said, pointing a thickened finger in the direction Karl had been heading where his new house was located. "And over there's a mix of shops catering to those hoity-toities and on the upper floors are the shopkeepers' apartments. I made anything from fancy bits of this and that for the noble dinner parties—tiny tartlets and bread in ridiculous shapes—to filled pastries for people who need to eat lunch on the go. But my specialty was anything with apples. They used to call me Mama Poma, back when the kids around here knew how to spell the word respect. These days they just break my windows and threaten to kill me if I don't hand them the rights to what is apparently prime real estate."

"Not the right time of year for apples," Karl replied, feeling a touch of déjà vu. "You make anything good with spring strawberries?"

Mama Poma snorted. "Hard to make something *bad* with strawberries. What's important is what you pair the berries with. A good pie crust is essential for strawberry-rhubarb pie."

"And a grasp of poisons," Karl added, but under his breath. Rhubarb could kill if prepared incorrectly.

She shot him a look that said she heard him and didn't appreciate the snark. Still, she stood and took a moment to dust her butt clean before turning the knob on the door behind her and heading inside.

"Well? You coming?"

Chapter Fourteen

KARL *KNEW* PIE crusts. Char had ensured Karl understood the ratios of flour to water and how essential it was to ensure he used cold butter. The feel of a crust coming together under Karl's hands, going from separate ingredients to the perfect flaky, doughy consistency as he mixed and kneaded was instinctive. In class he had instead focused on learning how to make the perfect filling for his already amazing crust, but one glance at Mama Poma as she worked dough underneath stiff fingers, and Karl immediately realized his folly. A true master was at work.

The berries and carefully sliced rhubarb were comfortably simmering in sugar, water, lemon juice, and a touch of corn starch. The heat would break down the fruit and the pectin would work with the corn starch to thicken the mixture into syrup. Karl abandoned the pot on the stove to hover next to Mama Poma. He memorized every twitch of her fingers as she incorporated the flour, every press of her palm to cut the butter into the dough, and even the moments she added more water, icy cold from the tap.

The ratios Karl was used to might be the same, and the basic technique was normal, too, yet even an untrained eye would be able to see how high quality her crust was in comparison to every other crust they had ever eaten.

Mama Poma set her crust aside to rest and turned to look at him, frowning. "Well? Show me what you can do."

Karl nodded. He had already washed his hands before starting on the filling, so he jumped right in. He measured out the flour, sprinkled in a little salt, and, since this was for a sweet pie, added a dash of sugar. He gently used his fingers to combine the flour mixture, checked the temperature of the water and the butter, which was already cut into perfectly sized chunks, and got to work.

Using the techniques Karl had learned from Char, and incorporating the gentle movements of Mama Poma, Karl let the dough speak to him.

"Slowly, boy. This isn't a race. You can't force cold butter to behave, or it will melt and ruin the consistency."

Karl obeyed, slowing his movements and almost immediately feeling the difference as his warm hands worked the cold ingredients into a dough. Mama Poma snorted and went to stir the simmering fruit.

The bakery was fairly spacious. The front room was dark behind the closed shutters but had a large display counter with enough space in front for customers to browse their options without stepping on one another. The doorway behind the counter led to the room Karl was working in. The entire left wall held ovens and stoves of many different sizes and various distances from the central heat of the fire to ensure perfect temperatures.

The strawberry-rhubarb filling continued to simmer on a midrange stove. The wall adjacent to the shop had floor-to-ceiling open shelving, except for right next to the door where there was a cold box. Every other space around the room, save for the opening for a back door and the wide sink on the righthand wall, was filled with spacious counters perfect for baking. Underneath the counters were deep cabinets containing all the mixing bowls and baking tools Karl needed. Spoons and spatulas hung from hooks in the walls. Basically, if Karl had to design his own bakery, it would look very similar to this.

He finished his dough and stepped back for Mama Poma to take a look. She stepped forward and gave the dough one knead, her palms firm as she pressed into the dough, before stepping back.

"Acceptable. I suppose you trained at that fancy school way up north?" she asked.

Karl nodded. "But my adoptive father taught me pie dough first," he added.

She studied him for a long moment, almost staring him down, arms crossed over her chest.

"Fine," she snapped out, shaking her head and sighing. "You're hired. I want two dozen chocolate chip cookies. You get started on that while I start up a custard. We'll use my dough for the pie and yours for custard tartlets. Well?" she added when Karl simply started at her, unsure how to answer that. Before yesterday and signing all those papers, he would have been absolutely thrilled. Now, he still wanted this. He so very badly wanted this. To hell with what all those hoity toity nobles thought. He would make cookies, and maybe some crusty rolls that could be split and filled with jam or cheese, and he would damned well enjoy it!

"Yes, Chef!" he replied, echoing the first lesson he remembered learning in the kitchen at Char's elbow. He was smiling ear to ear as he went to go find more sugar and butter to start creaming together to make his perfect chocolate chip cookies.

*

"I KNEW YOU'D be in a bakery!"

Karl jumped, jolted out of the meditative trance baking always induced, and some of the bread flour he had been carefully measuring out spilled onto the counter. He spun and saw Casmir leaning indolently against the jamb in the doorway to the kitchen, grinning. Except, the princely air he had adopted ever since he started living at the palace was gone. His clothes were ordinary homespun in simple brown pants and tan shirt. His hair was pulled back with a ribbon going tatty at the ends. Yet, it wasn't merely the clothes. Something about the tilt of his grin and the way he leaned said this wasn't Casmir, this was Ama.

"How'd you find me?" Karl asked. Mama Poma was over by the ovens, checking on the pie and tartlets. Ama had left the front door open on the far side of the shop, which revealed the street lights were still on even though light was starting to shine as the sun began to rise.

"Luckily the guards recorded your exit and one of them was paying enough attention to remember which direction you went in. From there it wasn't hard for me to figure out why you'd be walking toward the noble section of the city. And then I smelled delicious goodies wafting from this bakery, and I took a wild guess you'd be here."

Karl's cheeks heated, but he also couldn't help the rush that went through him at knowing Ama knew him well enough to have found him inside a random bakery out in the city. Except…

"Why were you looking for me? I don't have any appointments this early, do I?" The only reason anyone would be hunting him down so early in the morning was if something bad had happened.

Ama frowned and shook his head. "No one got hurt," he started, and the rushing feeling in Karl's gut turned into alarmed boiling. "Probably right around the time you were sneaking out, someone went to the palace kitchens and attacked Shan. Of course, Shan being Shan, he took care of the problem even before that dragon that's been trailing around the castle after him like a lost puppy came running."

Karl didn't even know where to start to begin unpacking everything Ama had just said. Since he knew Shan was okay—he was more skilled with knives than Karl, so the attacker hadn't stood a chance—Karl focused on the rest.

"A dragon has been harassing Shan?"

"I wouldn't call it harassing, per se," Ama replied, grinning, the twinkle in his eyes bright with mischief. "I heard this story secondhand, since I was still recuperating at the time the events actually occurred, but I heard Lyric and his sister Melody attended an informal dinner with the royal family. Lyric took one look at Shan and fell head over heels in love. Word is, Shan's not feeling harassed at all by the attention." He winked.

That was good to know, and Karl was happy for Shan, but the real reason he asked was because of Lyric. No matter how attuned he might be to Shan, Lyric had known about the attack early enough to get there before the guards could respond.

"Could they find any connection to Yaroi from what Shan left of the attacker?" Karl whispered so Mama Poma wouldn't overhear.

Ama shook his head. "Not a shred of evidence, but who else could it be? They probably learned one of Fen's sons was working in the kitchen and attacked. I assume they were targeting you, since you were on the mission in Yari, but got Shan instead. When you weren't in bed like you were supposed to be, some people got in a bit of a tizzy. I said I'd go find you, so here I am!" Ama bowed slightly at the waist, still grinning cheekily.

"Your hands can keep working even when your mouth is gabbing," Mama Poma called, scowling at them and glancing pointedly at Karl's dropped flour.

A laugh escaped Karl before he could suppress it, her words breaking through the seriousness of their conversation like a hot knife through butter. Karl obeyed, sweeping up the flour mess and starting to measure again.

"So attackers we believe were Yarokians were able to get into the castle and mount an attack, and Lyric the Yarokian prince knew about it ahead of time?" Karl asked, summing up everything Ama told him to ensure he had all the facts correct.

This certainly wasn't the first time assassins had gotten into the castle. Poor Uncle Caro had been attacked multiple times before he and Uncle Braxton were able to help Namin crown a new ruler. Every time a hole in the castle's security was discovered and plugged, somehow another one opened.

Karl added sugar and salt to the flour, mixing all the dry ingredients together even as his thoughts swirled. Next was oil and yeast from Mama Poma's starter. Karl let his hands do the work—the movements of mixing and adding more flour until a dough started to form automatic and not needing much thought—while his brain tried to work through the problem.

Ama, now known as Prince Casmir, was practically untouchable.

Attacking him meant war. Yaroi and Toval both had highly capable armies; war would ensure a bloodbath that would destabilize the rule of the current kings of each country. Regicide in a violence-prone society like Yaroi wasn't out of the question. Yaroi might be a power-based ruling system, but poison would kill dragon shifters just as easily as a rabbit shifter. The current king might have a lot of leeway, but he still needed to be careful. Yaroi would also want to keep in mind the consequences of getting Namin involved in the war. Killing or even just attacking Casmir would ensure the kingdom of prophesy would join on Toval's side.

No, Prince Casmir was safe. Karl pressed down on the dough, beginning to knead now that it had reached the right consistency.

Yaroi would see it as a waste of time to go after the soldiers involved in getting Melody out of Yari. They were simply following orders from those at the top. They might take a shot at Ralph because he commanded the mission, but at the moment the Royal Forces were in some unknown location training. If Karl didn't know where they were, Yaroi certainly didn't.

Which left Karl, who had been the one to rescue Ama, and was Fen's son. They could punish Fen for ordering his troops to go into Yari and punish Karl for his role simply by killing Karl. And, since Karl wasn't actually a proper prince of Toval, killing him would send the message Yaroi wanted without inciting war.

He pushed, turned, and pushed again, the dough gaining more elasticity with every knead.

"I'm the prime target, aren't I?" Karl asked Ama, who nodded and then shrugged.

"I'm sure they'd be happy to kill any of us, me in particular. You're just the easiest target, or so they think, at least. I know what you're capable of, and so does Prince Braxton or those guards wouldn't have let you out of the castle last night."

Karl sighed and patted the dough into a ball, dropping it into the bowl which he set aside on a different counter to proof for a while.

"So what next?"

Ama smirked. "They only said I should find you. They didn't say anything about bringing you back. I say you enjoy your baking for the morning, and when you're done we can go check out your new house. And if any of those damned Yarokians try anything against the two of us, they'll instantly regret it."

Karl snickered. "Don't think you get to just watch and relax all morning. Go wash your hands and find a big spoon. You get to mix the snickerdoodles I'm making next."

Ama opened his mouth to reply, already starting to roll up his right sleeve, but he suddenly snapped his mouth shut and spun to face the door, his hands raised in a defensive position in front of his face. A second later Karl heard what Ama must have: the scrape of footsteps on the stone stairs out front.

Chapter Fifteen

"HEY, YOU OLD hag!" a boy yelled. A moment later he stepped into the room.

About fifteen or sixteen, he had tan skin and long brown hair cut ragged at the shoulders. His clothes were roughly patched but fairly clean, so he was a wealthy enough street urchin. Or, he had learned the lesson that bad smells attracted attention, a death sentence for thieves mid-job. Three more kids followed him, two guys and a girl, all about the same age and the same level of cleanliness. All four were scowling and were doing their best to look tough and intimidating. Maybe in this neighborhood they were successful, but Karl had seen far worse during his time on the streets, and even more terrible acts of intimidation and force during his various stints with the army or when doing jobs for Braxton. Besides, from the way they walked with their balance on their heels, it was clear none of them were actual fighters. Again, maybe they had success in this hoity-toity neighborhood, but something felt off.

No Yarokian would be so weak. Perhaps they had been hired to flush Karl out so the Yarokians could find him? Why else would they be here? Karl stepped into open space so he could have room to pull his knives and fight.

"Didn't you hear what we said last time?" the boy continued, striding through the shop toward the kitchen. "Your baking days are over. Sell this place while you still can. We won't stop with breaking windows next time, and when there's nothing left, you won't earn a single copper penny."

Breaking windows? Mama Poma had mentioned something about that, hadn't she? Karl wracked his brain, trying to remember what she had said before he got distracted with baking. There had definitely been some-thing about breaking windows and refusing to sell. Which meant these wan-nabe ruffians were here for her, not for Karl.

Karl still didn't let his guard down. They might be wannabes, but he knew better than to be careless. Even the worst fighter got lucky at some point.

"It's my house and my business," Mama Poma snapped in reply. "Go bother someone else."

Blood near the food was unacceptable. Karl couldn't remember how many times Char had repeated that, particularly when soldiers, bloodied from battle, returned to camp. If Karl didn't want blood spilled in this kitchen, the situation needed to be deescalated fast.

He held up his hand perpendicular to his face, palm and fingers flat. When he was sure the boy was looking in his direction, Karl slowly bent his ring finger down in the thief's sign for just passing through. A street kid would know the sign and honor it.

But the kid just rolled his eyes and refocused on Mama Poma.

"All you need to do is sign this one piece of paper. You get the money, he gets his property, and everyone's happy."

Mama Poma snorted. "My answer hasn't changed. Go run back to your mommies."

"Then you leave us no choice," the boy declared. He reached behind him and pulled out a knife, but his movements were slow with inexperience and his grip on his knife wrong. This wasn't a street kid used to fighting for the merest scraps. He was probably a merchant or shopkeeper's son turned bully for hire. He could still do damage with that knife, though, so Karl let out a slow breath and let his hands drift down to where his own knives were hidden underneath his clothes.

"You picked the wrong day to attack this baker, kid," Karl said. "This is your last warning."

The kid let out a shout and charged, swinging his arm forward in a slash that probably would have bounced off Karl's collarbone, leaving only a bare nick in his skin … had Karl allowed the knife to land, of course. Karl yanked one of his own knives free and parried, hitting the kid's knife just right so it popped out of his hand and flew across the room. Karl shifted his weight and kicked, the sole of his right foot landing high on the kid's stomach.

The kid dropped to the ground, both hands pressed to his solar plexus as he gasped and gurgled, trying to get air.

A quick pivot and Karl dipped to the side to avoid the girl's slash, then dodged around the other two boys until he was behind them. Two kicks to the back of their knees and the boys were down. The girl shrieked and ran at him, knife raised high as if she planned to stab it downward into

Karl's skull. The knife wouldn't go through bone, of course. Maybe if she got lucky she'd hit Karl's eye or something else soft, but from the way her hand wavered in the air from the weight of the knife, she clearly didn't have the ability to aim that closely. Besides, if she actually hit anything, the knife was going to slide through her grip and slice her hand to ribbons, doing more damage to herself than her opponent. Karl mentally shook his head and then delivered another kick to the solar plexus. She dropped the knife as she hit the ground, joining her friend in gasping desperately for breath.

"If you're going to continue in this business, you need to learn more about your opponent before you blindly attack," Karl said. "Outside of the army, the two places where people know their way around knives are kitchens and bakeries. If Mama Poma were ten years younger, she would be the one standing here instead of me dressing you down. Now, pick yourself up and go back to whoever hired you and tell them to give up. Mama Poma isn't going to sell to them."

The kids scrambled to their feet and dashed off. The leader looked like he wanted to yell a parting insult, but it was taking all his breath just to run. They slammed the front door behind them.

Karl let out a breath and slid his knife back into the hidden sheath. Ama was leaning nonchalantly against the counter where Karl had sent him to get a spoon.

"Thanks for the help," Karl snarked.

Ama smirked and winked. "You didn't need my kind of help."

"Hah. I guess not." Karl grinned at him, sharing in the joke and enjoying the light flirting. "Let me wash my hands again, and we can get started on those cookies."

"You're no baker. You're military," Mama Poma said, stepping into the middle of the room.

"I'm not military," Karl replied, shaking his head. "But I started learning to bake in one of the kitchens in the military complex. Even bakers get dragged into military exercises, but I never enlisted. I went to Timmonsville, instead, for their two-year baking school."

"Right." Mama Poma eyed him, but she walked over to where his dough was proofing instead of asking any more questions. She poked a finger into the dough down to the first knuckle and pulled it free, then watched as the dough bounced back. "Well, you have some talent with baking at least, so not all of your story is a lie. At least tell me why you're really here."

"I have nothing to hide about that. I was just passing through and saw an old woman looking sad. It's only a lucky coincidence you run a bakery. I promise."

She harrumphed and went back over to the oven. "If that's the case, get those snickerdoodles made and those rolls done. Shop's opening in a little over an hour."

Karl obeyed. When he turned around, Ama was holding a spoon and looking hopeful. Karl laughed and waved him over.

"It's basic sugar cookie dough but with a ton of cinnamon. You'll like it."

"I'm sure I will," Ama replied.

They got to work, but this time Karl didn't fall into any sort of meditative trance while focused exclusively on the ingredients and the movements of his hands. Instead, he fell into joking with Ama until they both had flour on the ends of their noses. The cookies and the rolls took longer than they normally would have, but between Karl and Ama they managed to get it all done within Mama Poma's time limit.

About forty-five minutes after the bullies had left, a young woman came into the shop and started opening the shutters. She helped move the completed goods from the kitchen into the display cases out front.

"Should I make more?" Karl asked, surveying the mostly empty case. The pie, tartlets, bread, rolls, and cookies were a good start, but this bakery had space for double that, easily. Cakes and muffins, more types of pies, and even some of those hand pies Mama Poma had mentioned should fill the entire span of the case. Only having a couple shelves filled made it look somewhat sad.

Mama Poma frowned at him. "I have two cakes in the oven. You must have missed me making those." Her frown dipped into a scowl. "Lettia here is excellent with frosting and decorations, so she'll finish those up. This is more than I've been selling in years, so don't you worry your head about it. You were headed somewhere when you got waylaid by my moping. Go on, then."

"Thank you for the opportunity to bake here," Karl replied. He took off his apron and gave it to her, before following Ama outside into the morning sunlight. "You want to come with to check out my new house?"

"You know I do. Lead the way." Ama waved him on and Karl, feeling brave—or sugar high—took hold of Ama's hand. A moment later, Ama grinned and shifted so their fingers could tangle together. "Or we can walk together," Ama finished, squeezing his hand.

They didn't have far to go. The Whistfield city manor was only another block down the street. Karl had been closer than he thought before getting waylaid by the bakery.

Karl couldn't decide if he wanted the walk to be longer or shorter.

Walking hand in hand with Ama, even if it was the sugar rushing to his head that made him take such a brazen leap, was a pleasure. The heat of Ama's hand, the strength in his grip, and the way he smiled whenever Karl glanced at him was warmer than the taste of cinnamon still on Karl's tongue. Plus, the gentle squeeze of Ama's fingers intertwined with Karl's said quite clearly that Ama had no qualms about acting so intimately. Karl had spent far too much time suppressing his feelings for Ama, but the way Ama curled his fingers around Karl's said Karl might not have to suppress them any longer. Ama appeared to return Karl's affections and knowing that was sweeter than all the sugar Karl had baked with this morning combined.

Karl wanted to keep walking with Ama just like this. He wanted to put off the moment they reached the manor, and he had to let go of Ama's hand. If he were being honest, he also wanted to postpone the moment when he had to acknowledge being the lord of a manor. He had made a decision to do it, while staring at the back garden gate only a few hours ago, but the reality was still spine-shudderingly scary. He could walk into any kitchen anywhere in the world and be at home, but that was his past. His future, according to the still-wet ink on the papers he had signed, was the manor and everything it represented. The stabilizing comfort of holding Ama's hand helped Karl walk the last few feet down the street until they stopped at the front gate, which was pushed open wide enough for someone to squeeze through.

Karl had never seen the house from the front before, but it didn't look too bad. A bit of ivy crept up the walls and the gravel driveway was green with moss. Someone had been keeping up with basic maintenance outside, at least, or there would be baby trees and other weeds growing everywhere. Perhaps someone had cleaned up the inside too? Karl could only hope.

Karl let out a slow breath, grabbing for his courage. It was time to fully take on his new life as baron and embrace the manor and everything else too. He had decided, and he was resolved, and if his knees shook as he reached out with his free hand to push the gate wider, at least he was still moving forward.

"Okay—" Karl said, swallowing hard and gripping onto Ama's hand like the lifeline it was as he stepped through the gate and onto the gravel drive. "—let's go see what I'm in for."

Chapter Sixteen

"WHAT, YOU STALKING us now? Humiliating us once wasn't enough for you?"

Karl looked around at the general disarray, trying to find the familiar voice. The front garden wasn't as overgrown as the back, simply because the driveway dominated the space. From the gate, wide enough to drive a carriage through, the driveway went straight for about fifty yards before curving into an oval around a currently dry central fountain and more overgrown shrubbery. On the far side, the oval's curve flattened adjacent to the four grand marble stairs—currently brown with dirt—leading to a front door made of wood ornately carved with geometric shapes. The paint was chipped, but the lock looked sound. To the left were what Karl could only assume were gardens, given the massive overgrowth of bushes and flowerbeds left to go wild. To the right, along the fence that led behind the house, were outbuildings. What looked like an empty stable for maybe two horses, a gardener's shed, and a handful of other buildings, which Karl couldn't identify, were neatly tucked there. They had also once been painted and well cared for, but the paint was almost completely chipped away, leaving behind raw wood, starting to rot from exposure.

In front of the gardener's shed, the kid leader of the ineffectual group of thugs stood, glaring at Karl and Ama.

"You're denning here?" Karl asked, gaping at them. In all his years of being a street kid, he never would have dared come near a noble's house, even to steal from it. He certainly wouldn't have had the gumption to make his den there, and if he had, the noble would have sent him straight to jail for daring to try.

"Noble's dead," the kid scoffed. "No one lives here strong enough to order us off." His lip curled as he looked at the house. "Just some servants."

"I see." Karl glanced at Ama, who shrugged but also looked like he was holding in laughter. "It's not funny."

"It's hilarious," Ama retorted, a grin breaking out as his eyes sparkled. "A street thief owns the house, a street thug runs the grounds. Clearly there's nothing abnormal about any of this. Nothing funny at all."

He gave up on hiding behind cheap sarcasm and started laughing aloud, hands braced on his knees. Karl rolled his eyes, resisted the childish urge to push Ama into the dirt, and headed toward the front door. He knocked three times and then waited. No one came.

"You said there were servants living here?" Karl called over to the kid, who was gaping at him as if he didn't know what to make of Karl. Well, he probably didn't. Karl had been elbow deep in flour when he handily beat them, and now Karl was knocking on the front door of a noble's house like he belonged.

"They're probably hiding from the kids," Ama added before the kid could reply. "Luckily a certain someone passed me this before I left to search for you." He pulled a large brass key out of his pocket. "Shall we shock some servants before breakfast?"

He didn't wait for Karl to splutter out an answer, putting the key into the lock and turning it. The door opened with a squeal of old hinges, and Ama stepped aside so Karl could enter first.

"Who are you and what do you want from us? We don't have anything worth stealing!" someone called from the top of the stairs, her voice sharp with worry.

"Um…hi?" Karl tried to begin with, but then a man joined the woman, glared down at him, and started stomping down the stairs.

"We have enough trouble with those damned kids living in the gardening shed," he growled out. "I refuse to have someone invade the house as well!"

"Stop and think why we have the key," Ama—no, this authority wasn't Ama—Casmir snapped out. Casmir's body language had changed, his shoulders wide and exuding power as he settled back into his role as prince, yet his eyes still sparkled with mirth as he held out the key.

The man stopped halfway down the stairs, his mouth hanging open. "Are you the new Lord Whistfield?" he whispered, staring down at Casmir, who laughed in response.

"No, I'm Prince Casmir. He's your Lord Whistfield," Casmir finally said once he got his laughter under control, then pointed at Karl.

"P-prince! Your Highness, please excuse my rudeness," the man said, stuttering as his face turned pale. He sank to his knees in a bow, probably more because his knees no longer had the strength to hold him than because he intended to genuflect.

"Come now. We're the ones who must apologize for being rude," Casmir replied, waving the hand not holding the key as if brushing aside the bad feelings in the air. "We arrived early in the morning, much earlier than normal calling hours, and we neglected to send a note warning of our wish to view the property. Please, accept our apology." Casmir placed that free hand over his heart and bowed his head slightly.

Everyone remained like that for a few awkward seconds. The woman at the top of the stairs gaping at them, the man on the stairs bowing with one hand clutching the banister for balance, Casmir nodding, and Karl frantically trying to figure out something, anything, to say that might break up this standoff before it became even more uncomfortable.

"All right, what's all this ruckus?" a new woman called as she strode into the room from a doorway behind the stairs. She was older, at least fifty years old, and her graying hair was tied into a tight bun at the back of her head. An apron covered her dress, so she probably came from the kitchens. "It's too damn early for anyone to be whining!"

"He says he's the new prince," the woman at the top of the stairs explained, still sounding shocked. "He and the new baron are here."

"Does he now?" the new woman said, turning her glare on Casmir and Karl. "I've worked for spoiled brat nobles going on thirty years now. Never known of one to *walk* to their house, let alone wear such shabby clothing." She sniffed. "You're not the first to pretend to be the rightful owner of this house, and I doubt you'll be the last. You will leave now."

"Madam, I assure you—"

"Leave. Now," she said, cutting Casmir off sharply as she pointed at the door.

Casmir glanced over at Karl and wrinkled his nose. His eyes were still twinkling with laughter, the damned brat, because clearly this was all a big joke to him. Which, okay, it was kind of funny being treated like the thieves they were. It was also definitely Karl's fault to have arrived dressed like a common person rather than a noble. This would be easy enough to fix: go back to the palace and put on proper clothes, then arrive back at the house in a carriage with all the notarized paperwork stating he did have a rightful claim to be here. Of course, the second he stepped back into the palace, everyone would be all over him to have guards and protection and whatnot. There would be meetings and no doubt other tedious things he would get dragged into, and it could be days before he had another chance to come back. Yet, he couldn't think of any other way to change these servants' minds.

Casmir apparently came to the same conclusion because he rolled his eyes at Karl and turned to the door.

As if on cue, a clatter of carriage wheels and the stomp of booted feet echoed through the open front door as a retinue arrived.

"Now, that will be our actual lord," the older woman snapped out.

"You mean, they actually found someone?" the man asked, rising to his feet and walking down the rest of the stairs.

"I told you they had, and that he would be arriving in the next day or so. At least it sounds like he'll have guards to arrest these fakers," she added with a glare at Casmir and Karl.

A minute later Braxton strode through the front door, and Karl smiled, relieved to see him.

"Well, the outside needs some work, but the inside doesn't look too bad," Braxton said as he looked around the foyer. He looked over at Karl.

"I'll send some gardeners over to at least get started on clearing away the mess out there until you're able to hire permanent staff for that."

"I appreciate it," Karl replied.

Braxton nodded and walked over, brushing a white-gloved hand through Karl's hair. "You have flour in your hair again. Have you been to see the kitchen here yet? I heard it's a decent size."

"Haven't gotten past the doorway," Casmir replied, his tone sardonic, yet cheeky at the same time.

"We, uh, had a bit of trouble," Karl added.

"That's what you get for sneaking out of the palace at a ridiculous hour of the morning in street clothes," Braxton replied, bopping him gently on the top of the head with a loose fist. "Right." He clapped his hands as he turned to the three servants, all of whom were staring at Braxton with their mouths open. "This is Lord Karlow Musen Whist, Baron Whistfield." He waved at Karl. "This is His Highness, Prince Casmir Sventoval. I am Prince Braxton Tovalian. And this is the paperwork declaring Karl as the rightful heir of Whistfield," he finished, waving to someone outside, who hurried in carrying a fat folder full of papers. "We've come to assess the state of the house, hire on full staff, and make ready for Karl to move in."

All three servants gaped a moment longer before belatedly dropping to their knees in a deep bow.

"None of that," Braxton called, already walking past them to the stairs. "We have far too much to do, and I need to get back to the palace in time for a lunch meeting I can't miss. Let's go!" he called in the direction of the open doorway.

First inside was Shan, closely followed by Lyric, and after them came a stream of people who dispersed throughout the house.

"Are you okay?" Karl asked, hurrying over to Shan. "I heard about the attack."

Shan grinned. "Not a scratch on me, but Uncle Terrance is pretty glad I'm moving here instead. He didn't appreciate the assassins disrupting his meal prep last night. And then Lyric ran into the room and knocked some stuff over. When Uncle Braxton said you'd be needing a sous chef here, I was happy to take the job."

"I'm not hiring my own brother as my servant!" Karl yelped out.

Shan laughed. "As if you won't be spending more time in your own kitchen than me. This is what I want to do. I'm just lucky my brother has the chance to make it happen for me."

Karl frowned at him, glancing from Shan's hopeful expression up to Lyric's frowning one.

"I doubt I'll be able to accommodate you at the level of luxury you prefer," Karl said to Lyric. Ama's words earlier about how Lyric rushed to Shan's side, and the way Lyric was hovering protectively over Shan now was very indicative of Lyric's intentions. Shan looked up at Lyric after Karl's warning, and the way his eyes shone as their gazes connected said Shan returned Lyric's attentions.

"Quieter here," Lyric replied. "I'm not really a Prince of Yaroi any longer, since I've defected, so it's better for me to be here with Shan than in the palace."

"He's right, you know," Casmir added, dropping an arm over Karl's shoulder as he joined them. The warmth and comfort of that arm was addicting, and Karl wanted to snuggle closer to feel more of Casmir's body against his. Only Shan's knowing smirk kept Karl still.

"What is he right about?" Karl asked, forcing his mind to stay on task.

"You're going to be holding meetings with other nobles and important people elbow deep in flour in the kitchen. I can see it now."

"As if!" Karl elbowed Casmir in the stomach, and his arm dropped away from Karl's shoulders to protectively cover his midriff. "But I guess it wouldn't hurt to go see the kitchens now, right?"

"Right," Shan replied, grinning.

Karl turned to look at the three servants, who were still standing in the middle of the foyer, mouths dropped open. "Are the kitchens this way?" he asked, pointing toward the door under the stairs.

"N-no, my lord," the older woman said. "I mean, yes my lord, but that's the servant's halls."

"Is there any way to get to the kitchen without going through the servant's halls?" Karl asked. "And don't call me my lord. I'm Karl."

"Um, no, my— um, Lord Karl. The kitchens are close to the dining room, though, so we could go through there instead?"

"Lead the way, then, please," Karl replied, smiling at her. "I'm afraid you're just going to have to get used to us," he added as she started walking. "We're an odd bunch, for nobles. What's your name, by the way?"

"I'm Leslie, Lord Karl. I'm a kitchen servant. Stephanie is your chambermaid, and Gerald is your manservant. There used to be more servants, of course, but the estate only needed us three on staff while they searched for the new lord."

"Nice to meet you, Leslie. It sounds like Uncle Braxton is working on fixing the servants issue—" *He had probably corralled the street urchins in the gardening shed and likely hired them as house laborers, which was going to be interesting.*

"—so we should have a full house again in no time." And for the first time, Karl found himself looking forward to his future here. With Casmir and Shan at his side, he was actually starting to believe suddenly becoming a baron wasn't going to be too bad.

Chapter Seventeen

A WEEK CERTAINLY wasn't long enough to call anything part of a routine. Karl knew that. He was also perfectly aware that the entire week had been very lenient on him. As baron, there were social engagements and actual responsibilities he had been shamelessly shirking, using the excuse he was still setting up his household. That excuse wouldn't last for much longer, especially since he was basically done hiring servants and secretaries and all the other people he now needed to employ, thanks to being one of the wealthiest and most influential nobles in the kingdom. He hadn't really gotten to delve into what that meant in terms of estates and the taxes he collected from the port; his focus this week was mainly on what he needed for the city house and to be able to move through the court like he belonged.

Casmir and Lyric had both conspired to update Karl's wardrobe, including his jewelry, and the massive attached closet in his bedroom was slowly filling with all kinds of outfits as the tailors Casmir commissioned delivered their work. Shan had gone from sous chef to head chef, mostly due to the fact that he was the only one aside from Karl who actually knew how to run a kitchen, and he was thriving. In addition to Leslie, Shan had hired two more staff for cooking and two for serving, plus a pastry chef in training since Karl spent a couple hours every day baking.

Somehow, amid all of that chaos, Karl managed to develop a routine that wasn't old enough or solidified enough to actually be called a routine. Around three every morning, Karl woke and snuck out of the house, heading to Mama Poma's. She was a phenomenal teacher, giving him some one-on-one, hands-on depth Timmonsville had never been able to offer. When the shop girl arrived around six, Karl left, returning home to his own kitchen, where he scared Leslie and made Shan roll his eyes because he made the bread for breakfast. And muffins, and some pastry crust when Shan and Michael—the assistant pastry chef—thought some sort of pie might be needed that day. Karl also made rolls for lunch and something sweet so everyone in the household could have a bit of yum.

Breakfast was next, in the dining room with whomever was awake— usually Lyric and Casmir. After, Karl went to his office where he reviewed and signed paperwork, interviewed for open positions, and did whatever other office work was needed. Then lunch, and afterward Casmir dragged him into the backyard, which had somehow gotten cleared and re-sodded, where they sparred for a bit to make up for all the desk work. There really was nothing quite like the gleam in Casmir's eyes—or, technically Ama's eyes, since he dropped Casmir and became Ama whenever they were facing each other, wooden training knives in hand. Karl dreamed about that gleam in those so very bright hazel eyes, dreams he muffled into his pillow to keep anyone from overhearing, particularly Casmir.

Somehow, Casmir had conned his way into getting the spouse's suite of rooms, which shared an attached door to Karl's suite. Finding out Casmir had heard Karl whenever Karl had one of those dreams would be mortifying. Particularly since the implications of why Casmir had chosen the spouse's rooms was…something Karl wouldn't dwell on at the moment. He had too much else to worry about than where his feelings for Casmir might be going.

Karl sighed and rolled over in bed. At least, he ought to have too much else to worry about, and yet his thoughts on the matter had jolted him awake a full twenty minutes early. He could have slept for longer, yet here he was, staring at the ceiling, thinking about Casmir sleeping comfortably in the next room.

What would Casmir say if Karl tried to proposition him? Karl stifled a gasp, his cheeks heating at just the thought, and he buried his face into his pillow. Karl could already imagine how awkward and stuttering he would be if he ever found the gumption to try. Besides, he liked the friendship they had now and didn't want to do anything to jeopardize it.

What was best for them both was for Karl to stick to the routine, which meant he might as well get up and go to the bakery. Karl rubbed one hand down his face and then sat up, the blankets pooling in his lap. His bedroom was dark, the shades over the window drawn to block the moonlight and any streetlamps. The curtains around his four-poster were tied back, though, since he didn't need their protective warmth as spring began to heat into summer. The room wasn't too different to the room he had back in the palace: opulent by his standards but simple in comparison to what he assumed most nobles wanted. The bed dominated the room, a massive mattress set into the four-poster frame. In the darkness, Karl couldn't see the pale wood that matched perfectly with the green blanket he chose, nor the matching pale wood tables on either side of the bed where he had some mage-light lamps. The windows were on the wall to Karl's right, and on his left, the door into his sitting room and the rest of the house. Directly across was a wide fireplace with doors on either side. The left door led into his closet and dressing room, and a door inside there led into Casmir's closet and dressing room. The right door led into his private bathing room. At some point, plumbing had been added to the house but no running water. Karl had to pump his own water, but the fact that there was even a pump at all put this house eons ahead most others in the city. It wouldn't cost too much more to hire magical engineers to turn the pumps into running water spigots, so that was the first item on his renovations list now that all the old furniture from the previous owner had been removed and Karl's preferred furniture delivered.

There was still so much to do. Too much. Karl didn't want to dwell on it, so instead, he swung his legs off the bed and stood, heading to his dressing room where Jeff, Karl's new manservant, had laid out the nondescript clothing Karl wore to the bakery. He only took a few minutes to get dressed and then quietly went through his sitting room and out into the hallway outside the bedrooms. Karl had the largest room, followed by Casmir's, whose door was next on the hallway. Shan and Lyric shared the room directly across from Casmir's. Lyric originally had the now-empty room next to Shan's, but he never used it and had eventually given up the pretense. The servants had their own private wing, much better for the kids who had been sleeping in the gardener's shed, and the rest of the rooms were empty, set up as guest rooms. Braxton had stayed over once, but aside from him, any other visitors Karl would have welcomed were still off somewhere mysterious.

He stayed quiet as he padded down the carpeted hallway and down the stairs, nodding to the guards stationed inside the doors, one of whom pulled the front door open for him. Outside the doors, gentle night air blew and clouds scudded across the star-strewn sky. Another pair of guards stood outside the doors, two more were stationed inside the closed and locked gates, and another two were outside the gates, and that was only the guards in the front of the house. Plus, there were additional guards not in plain sight. Braxton wasn't taking any chances. Karl felt safe in assuming the route he took to and from the bakery every morning was well-guarded as well. He still kept his eyes and ears open as the guards relocked the gate behind him. He walked through the night-darkened streets, but only the crickets greeted him for the couple blocks he needed to travel.

He climbed the stairs and let himself into the bakery, the door unlocked like usual. The lights were off in the storefront, but the back was well lit.

"There you are," Mama Poma grumbled at him, scowling, as he walked through the entryway and into the bright lights of the kitchen. "Thanks to you, we've been going through the stock in the pantry. I did some reorganizing last night, and I found these." She thrust a bowl at him, the contents sloshing. Slices of partially rehydrated dried apples soaking in what smelled like water, nutmeg, cinnamon, allspice, and a touch of wine filled the bowl almost to the brim. "Another hour and those will be useable again," she continued, walking over to the prep station Karl preferred. "Which means I get to teach you my world-famous apple bread recipe today."

"You can?" Karl asked, excitement growing as he joined her at the counter. He placed the bowl carefully out of the way, his attention fixed on her. She had said over and over that she was famous for any baked recipes that included apples, and he believed her. The first apples wouldn't be ready for picking for months, so Karl had instead focused on learning the rest of her techniques so he would be ready to absorb the remainder this fall. She was a master, and Karl was honored she was willing to teach him. Finding dried apples in the spring was an unlooked for but very welcome bonus!

She snorted at him. "No, I'm reconstituting apples to make another strawberry pie." She rolled her eyes and pulled over an empty bowl. "Dry ingredients." She pulled over a larger bowl. "Wet ingredients. Let's do this."

Karl quickly washed his hands, found an apron, and then started measuring out the dry ingredients. He started with the flour, carefully leveling out the measuring cup.

"No yeast?" he asked, surprised, when the next two ingredients proved to be baking soda *and* baking powder, which, along with the eggs, were all that would provide leavening in this recipe.

"Not in this recipe," she replied, passing him the ginger and cinnamon. "It's an easy recipe that anyone can make but tastes like it's professional bakery level. That's why I'm showing it to you now, then waiting until we have real apples for the rest of my repertoire."

"Then I'll look forward to autumn," Karl said, grinning as he added the salt and carefully mixed all the dry ingredients together. He switched to the larger bowl and started cracking eggs. White sugar, brown sugar, vanilla, and oil, and the second bowl was ready too. All that was left were the apples.

"They're already peeled and cored. We just need to chop them into chunks. I'll start on that if you want to work on incorporating the dry ingredients into the wet?" She pulled out a paring knife and reached into the bowl to find one of the plumper chunks of rehydrated apple.

"Sounds good." Karl grinned, humming to himself as he located a spatula and poured some of the flour mixture into the egg mixture and got to work.

Interlude

TODAY HE FELT like Ama rather than Casmir. Ama couldn't have said why, only that here in the luxury of Karl's house he didn't have to stuff himself back into the veneer of Casmir on days when being Ama felt more natural. Karl completely understood and somehow never mixed up which name Ama was using at any given moment. He could see through Ama that clearly, could read him like no one else ever could before. This was clearly paradise, and Ama was loving every single second of it. Or, at least, he should be.

He rolled out of bed and stretched, lifting his arms over his head and lacing his fingers together to loosen his shoulders and back. He dropped his arms back to his sides and let out a contented sigh as he headed to his dressing room to find clothing for the day.

Casmir liked the fancier clothes with bright colors and intricate embroidery. Ama preferred subdued colors in simpler designs, closer to what common people wore throughout the city and certainly not appropriate for a prince to be wearing. He chose simple brown pants and a deep blue shirt, no vests, jackets, or any other accoutrements needed and discarded his sleeping clothes into the basket for the servants to take care of before getting dressed. The entire time, that closed door leading between his room and Karl's taunted him.

Ama's life here in Karl's house was so very close to being perfect. All he was missing was that one last thing—the one thing his heart yearned for, yet he didn't dare reach out to take. He wanted Karl.

He wanted Karl's body, of course. The man was gorgeous, his smile infectious, and he was deadly with his knives. But Ama also desperately wanted Karl's heart too. He wanted Karl to return his affections, which didn't seem possible. Karl was so busy figuring out how to be a baron. Learning all his new responsibilities, his new status, and what all that meant in the larger picture of his life was so completely overwhelming for him that Ama didn't dare intrude with the inconvenience of sharing his feelings.

Instead, Ama did what he could to support Karl from the shadows, exactly how he'd lived his life to this point. The guards all around the house might be supplied by Braxton, but Ama was the one in charge of security. He did placements and rosters, installed the sniper's nest on the roof and the tactical positions hidden in the street outside. Karl needed to bake. Not just as a way to relieve stress, but also because it was simply a part of him. He *needed* dough between his fingers and flour in his hair the way Ama needed the reassurance of the press of the knife sheathed against his lower back. Ama did everything he could to ensure Karl could go to that bakery every morning and had more plans in place to help Karl fit in even more baking if possible.

Ama left his room and headed downstairs, going to the kitchen so he could grab something to eat while he waited for Karl to return. The sunlight was a bare glimmer on the horizon, still a good hour or so off from actually rising, but the morning birds were out in force, chirping loudly out in the garden where the new gardeners were already hard at work doing what they could to beat back the overgrowth and return the gardens to any sort of splendor. Karl said when he last visited this house—sneaking in through the back—the gardens hadn't been overgrown, but they hadn't been pretty either. Ama was fairly certain the gardeners wouldn't rest until Karl had the nicest yard in the city. One of the street urchins had taken to gardening, and he was out there toiling away, looking incredibly happy. One of the other boys had taken Braxton's offer and joined the army. The girl had chosen to become a maid here. And the leader was shaping up to be a fine butler. All three who had chosen to stay were also learning some other lessons from Ama, ones where they could put their street thug ways to better use should the need arise. The gardening shed was back to being used for its original purpose, at least.

Ama shook his head and left the window, continuing his trek to the kitchen. In most nobles' houses a parlor or smoking room was the center of their household, and any business was conducted in an office. That wouldn't work for Karl. They had an engineer coming by tomorrow to assess the wall separating the kitchen from the storeroom on the other side. Ama hoped they could remove the wall entirely, thereby expanding the kitchen and adding a proper baker's area as well as a formal desk. Sometime in the future, Karl would be receiving callers down here, wearing an apron and covered in flour, so he needed a desk. Plus, he could make something and while he was waiting for it to rise or to bake, he could sit at his desk and complete his work as a baron at the same time. Ama wanted to make being baron as easy for Karl as possible, so he was going to press that engineer hard to find a solution that made that wall disappear. Plus, they weren't going to lose storage space as the dungeon was only one flight down from the wine cellar. Karl had ordered it be used for storage instead, after it was thoroughly scrubbed. Ama hadn't known nobles' houses came with dungeons and couldn't fathom why it had been installed in the first place, but he had gotten the story about how Karl knew about said dungeon, so had a good idea of what it was used for. Now, it would be used to store flour and sugar instead.

"Hey, Will. Hey, Leslie," Ama called as he walked into the kitchen and saw Leslie was already busy at the stove and Will was halfway through a plate of eggs and toast.

"Master Ama," Leslie and Will replied, Will slurring through a mouthful of food.

"How are you this morning?" Leslie asked after giving Will a dark look. "What would you like for breakfast?"

"Whatever you're making will be delicious, I'm sure," Ama replied, settling onto the kitchen stool next to Will. "Anything I should know about for today?"

"Nothing unusual," Leslie replied, plating eggs for him as she spoke. "I'm expecting the normal courier from the palace with today's work for Master Karl any minute, and the shipment of baking equipment is supposed to arrive today at some point too. As soon as Master Karl returns from the bakery, I'm sure there will be far too much work for him again."

"He must really love baking," Will said. He was using his toast to push more eggs onto his fork, ignoring the knife at his place setting.

Shan laughed as he walked into the room. He didn't handle breakfast for the household. He and Leslie worked lunch together, and then he took over the kitchen for dinner while she rested. Lyric would still be asleep for at least another couple hours, but that didn't stop Shan from coming down most mornings to have breakfast with everyone else.

"He and I are Musens. You have to have cooking coursing through your veins to be a Musen, you know. Char wouldn't have been allowed to adopt us into the family if we didn't. From what I understand, at least. From living with Char for so long, I can tell you Karl's pretty normal in comparison to the rest of the Musen clan."

Ama would have read some negative subtext about Shan talking about himself, if he didn't know Shan was just as nuts about cooking and quite happy with running Karl's kitchen. Instead he tucked into the plate of food Leslie delivered.

"I'm just glad someone's using that old bakery where Master Karl goes every morning," Leslie said as she returned to the stove to start plating Shan's portion. "Since the old lady who owned it died six months back, the place has been sitting empty. Kind of sad, really."

"Empty?" Ama said, slowly lowering his fork to place it on the table, worry starting to churn in his gut. "What do you mean, empty?"

"Yeah, who's the old lady we got hired to rough up then?" Will added, looking confused.

Hired by someone Braxton hadn't been able to track down, Ama added, mentally connecting some dots as panic began to set in. Ama tried to keep himself calm by telling himself Karl had been going to that bakery every morning for the last week by himself with no issues. There was no reason to believe today would be any different.

But, if Ama were trying to lay a trap designed to capture Karl, putting an old lady in trouble and a failing bakery in Karl's path was exactly what Ama would have done. Since a week had gone by, Ama hoped the enemy were still setting up their plot; there could still be time to save Karl. Or, they were waiting for another chance to grab both Karl and Ama at the same time. They knew Ama had joined Karl at the bakery once, when they were still laying the foundation of their trap, so maybe they were waiting for Ama to appear again?

"We have to go get him!" Shan gasped, standing so quickly his stool went tumbling back. "We should gather the guards and storm the building!"

"I'll grab everyone!" Will added, sending his own stool flying as he headed for the door.

Ama reached out and grabbed Will by the shoulder, holding his other hand up to stop Shan.

"Wait. Wait," Ama said slowly as his thoughts solidified. "This is definitely a trap, most likely laid by Yaroi to punish us all. Lyric is here, and if Karl escapes he'll run here, so we have to defend this as our base. Shan, I need you and Lyric stationed here with most of the guards. I'll take some of the hidden guards with me, so this place will still look fully defended. Will, I need you to get to the palace and alert Prince Braxton and get us some more backup."

Ama looked around the room, catching everyone's eyes. "Let's go."

Everyone scattered, Ama checking all his weapons were in place, desperately hoping he would make it in time.

Chapter Eighteen

"IS THAT ALL mixed?" Mama Poma asked, glancing over Karl's shoulder at the bowl where he had just finished incorporating the dry ingredients into the wet. She took the spatula out of Karl's hand and gave the bowl a stir, nodding when she didn't see any clumps of flour. "Good. I'll go oil the loaf pan. You mix those apple chunks in. We'll get this in the oven, and then you can start on the bread while it bakes. Eating it will be a good reward for all our efforts this last week." She smirked at him, then turned away to dig through the cabinet with all the bakeware.

Karl left her to it, bringing the bowl over to the cutting board where she had left the apples in even-sized, small chunks. Her knife skills were remarkable. Karl picked up a handful of apples and moved to toss them into the bowl, when his magic suddenly pinged.

Karl didn't need to focus on his magic while working. It was always there, passively in the background where he could forget about it, though he did use it to be a better baker on occasion. Red magic might be death magic, but that didn't mean he only had to use it to hurt or kill. He was particularly good at using it to keep yeast healthy and ready to bloom. However, having red magic wasn't something he was ready to advertise. Outside of missions for Braxton, Karl generally pretended he didn't have magic at all. That didn't mean the magic forgot about him though.

Karl let his magic play out as it wanted, turning his body so he was between the red glow and where Mama Poma stood digging through the cabinet, muttering angrily to herself. His magic settled onto the apples, digging through their components. Apple, some of the magic used in the drying process, cinnamon, nutmeg, ginger. For a moment, his magic fluttered around the hint of the wine used to rehydrate the apples, wanting to decay the alcohol, but then something else caught its attention. Astringent, like the cleansing solution healers liked to use, and bitter like arugula. Definitely not something that should be mixed in with apples.

Karl glanced over his shoulder at Mama Poma, who had a stack of baking trays and cake pans on the floor next to her as she dug for the loaf pan. She wasn't looking in his direction. Karl tightened his grip on his magic, focusing it from simple pinging to directed discovery. After a moment, Karl was certain. A sleeping potion had been poured over the apples, one that would resist the heat of the oven. One bite of the bread when Mama Poma served it, and he would sleep until someone administered the counterspell.

Decaying the potion would be simple for him, but Karl hesitated, glancing over his shoulder again. The pile of sheet trays had grown, but no bread tin had apparently been located. Mama Poma swore softly as she dug some more.

Where had she gotten the apples? Were they lost in the pantry like she claimed, or was this instead another ploy by a different set of thugs to force her into selling the bakery? All they had to do was wait for her to taste a baked good made from the apples, and they could kidnap her easily.

Karl opened his mouth to warn her, but she swore again and then let out an angry, animalistic snort, and he snapped his mouth shut. That hadn't sounded human. In all the time Karl had been around her, he'd never caught her scenting the air or tilting her head to hear better, or any other traits that indicated half of her was some sort of animal. But then, a spy would be trained not to give something so obvious away, particularly a Yarokian spy.

The potion might be aimed at kidnapping him instead. Karl frowned in thought, then blasted the apples. The potion immediately decayed down to nothing, and so did the alcohol. The apples had, luckily, already been dried and were therefore much more resistant to decay. They lost some of the plumpness from rehydration and the edges turned brown, but the potion was destroyed before the apples were harmed too much. Karl stopped his magic and finished scooping the apples into the batter, carefully mixing them all together.

"Damned thing had fallen behind the shelf," Mama Poma snarled out, thrusting the loaf pan at him. "Oil that, pour the batter in, and dust the top with some sugar, then shove it in the oven. I'll clean up the mess I just made." She returned to the cabinet, which looked empty inside since all the bakeware was scattered on the floor around it.

Karl followed her directions, but his hands moved automatically as he poured some oil in the pan and tilted it to get the oil to spread and cover every surface. If Mama Poma was a Yarokian spy like he suspected, then why wait a week to spring this trap? They must have needed the time to prepare and get assets in place. Drugging Karl would mean nothing if they didn't have a means to then move him to a secured location. A week was also enough time to set up a pattern—a damned routine, which was exactly what he had been thinking about just that morning. Ama and all of Karl's guards had been on alert every time Karl headed to the bakery, but after a week they wouldn't be worried about him until he didn't return to the house at his usual time. That gave Mama Poma a secure window to act within.

They also knew about Ama, Karl realized with dawning horror. When Karl had been out and about during the botched attack on the palace, Ama was the one who had responded. If their real goal was to get Ama, they didn't even need to move Karl. They just had to keep him drugged and out of commission so he couldn't help, and Ama would blithely walk into their trap in his search for Karl. Ama might be incredibly strong, but one man against however many assets Mama Poma had brought into the city didn't stand a chance.

Karl was the one who had to save himself, and thereby, also save Ama.

Decided, Karl wiped out the excess oil and poured the batter into the pan. He smoothed the top with the spatula, and then scooped a spoonful of sugar and carefully dusted the top. Once the pan was ready, Karl slid it into the oven.

"How long does it bake for?" he asked.

"Hmm?" Mama Poma looked up from where she was organizing sheet trays and saw he was standing next to the oven. "Oh, forty minutes. It's only one loaf, but it's a wet batter."

Karl nodded and returned to his station. So he had forty minutes to come up with a plan. He moved all the dirtied dishes to the sink and wiped down the countertop, before pulling the flour close. He always thought better while kneading, and Mama Poma had told him to get started on some rolls after the apple bread.

The easiest plan was to incapacitate Mama Poma and make a run for it. He had the element of surprise, and if he started yelling the second he went out the front door the guards hidden in the street outside would respond. They might capture Mama Poma, but the rest of the Yarokai in the city would escape and be able to come up with a new plot. Running was a short-term solution, but a longer-term mess. Karl wanted to end the actual threat, not prolong it.

His other option was to pretend to be knocked out by the potion. He would wait for Ama to arrive, and then it would be two against however many, and he and Ama could both die together.

Karl grimaced, looking at his hands, manipulating what was slowly becoming a sticky glop of dough as the ingredients melded. He added more flour and dug his fingers back in. Pretending to be afflicted by the potion was still the better option, since he could always get up and try running if the situation changed. He didn't have an ideal plan, but it was better than nothing.

Karl set his dough aside to rest and went to wash his hands. He spent some time tackling the pile of dirty dishes in the sink, scrubbing away all the cooking residue and lining all the dishes up on a drying rack. By the time the sink was empty again, the bakery sang with the warm scents of cinnamon and nutmeg perfuming the air. The apple bread was done. Karl found cloth to protect his hands and pulled the loaf pan from the oven. The tin went onto a cooling rack, the bread still too hot to remove, but it smelled divine. The bread had risen all the way to the top of the tin and cinnamon and nutmeg-scented steam drifted lazily upward from the crispy browned top. If Karl didn't know the apples were subpar, he would have thought it a perfect loaf of bread and been looking forward to trying it.

He started work on a batch of cookies while the bread cooled, creaming together butter and sugar before adding the vanilla and eggs. He was beginning to measure out flour for the dry ingredients when Mama Poma came over, the apple bread out of the tin and resting centered on the cutting board in her hands.

"I think it's cool enough to try now," she said, carefully setting the board down on the counter next to him. She went to the other counter to retrieve a serrated bread knife, then returned a moment later, handing it to him hilt first.

"I'm looking forward to it," Karl lied, but he obeyed her silent command and put the knife to the bread. He cut the heel off and then sliced twice more. The inside was moist and fluffy, a really good crumb without being mushy. Fresh apples would have added to the moisture, but he wasn't upset with how the texture had turned out. Karl handed Mama Poma a slice and picked up the second one for himself.

"Go on," Mama Poma said, urging him along with a smile, her slice of bread seemingly forgotten in her hand. "I want to know what you think!"

There was no turning back once he put the bread in his mouth. Karl steeled his nerve and his resolve, brought the slice to his mouth, and took a bite.

Brilliant spices bloomed across his tongue, the cinnamon and nutmeg he'd smelled earlier melding seamlessly with the apple. The crumb of the bread was as soft as it looked, a perfect conveyance for the spice. However, the apples themselves… If Karl's magic hadn't already told him something was wrong, tasting Mama Poma's alleged signature dish with these apples would have alerted him. The apples were chewy and gummy. They imparted apple flavor, but the texture did not match with the crumb of the bread at all. Fresh apples were clearly the only viable option for this recipe.

"Well?" Mama Poma asked, looking at him expectantly. Yet, the tilt to her head as she studied him said she was expectant for more than just his opinion on the bread. It was time for his acting skills to be put to work.

"Delicious," Karl said. "I need—" He frowned and dropped the rest of the bread onto the cutting board as he staggered and used that hand to brace himself. "—the recipe." He forced the words out as if his thoughts were merely slowed and he didn't realize he was speaking in short gasps. His hand slid off the counter as he sank to his knees. "Wha…?" he slurred, blinking up at Mama Poma.

She stood over him, a slight smile lifting her lips. "Don't worry, little princeling. You'll only sleep for a bit. Your real punishment won't start until you wake back in Yaroi. Have a good nap." She turned away, heading to the back door, which she threw open. A moment later, two men Karl didn't recognize walked into the room, heading for where Karl lay on the floor, slumped against the cabinets. The bright, gleeful and spiteful light in their eyes said they weren't thinking about him surviving all the way back to Yaroi. In fact, they probably weren't interested in his live body leaving this bakery at all.

Chapter Nineteen

THE KNIVES HIDDEN up Karl's sleeves slid into his hands with practiced ease. He squinted up at the two men through eyelids opened just enough for him to see. When one leaned close, Karl slashed. Skin and muscle parted like a hot knife through butter as Karl slit his throat. The other was only close enough for a stab in the leg, but Karl aimed for the femoral artery. He didn't know if he hit it, but the man screamed in pain and fell to the ground clutching his leg all the same. Karl sprang to his feet just in time for six more men to dash into the room. One on six wasn't great odds, especially now the element of surprise was gone, but Karl wasn't ready to show all his tricks just yet by adding his magic to the mix. He stuck to the corner, even though the two bodies got in the way of his footing—the rest of the attackers couldn't get to his back that way—and brandished his knives.

"This all you got?" Karl called, goading them.

The closest attacker, a woman in dark leather, snarled and dashed forward with her sword at the ready, one of the men was a step to her right, his own short sword already slashing. Karl caught the blade of the man's sword where blade met guard on his knife, turning it aside, and simultaneously kicked out at the woman. She dodged back and Karl pushed with his knife, turning the man into her path. They tangled for a brief moment, just long enough for Karl's knife to kiss the wrist of the man. Blood gushed, fountaining in pulsing jets over all three of them, but as the man fell, another took his place.

Five on one, but the remaining five were more cautious now. They spread out so they wouldn't hamper one another. This time, when two lunged forward they were on opposite sides. Karl slashed to his left, trying to slow that one down while lunging out of the way of the man on his right. Metal clanged again and Karl gritted his teeth as the painful shot from the jar of the knife in his right hand flashed up his arm. He focused to his right for a brief second, freeing his blade from entanglement with the attacker's short sword, then stepped into a slash that had the man scrambling back, but that left his left side unguarded.

Piercing pain radiated up his left arm, locking his shoulder, then moved down, making his fingers go limp. His knife clattered to the floor and Karl pressed his back against the wall, not sure if he dared to look at the damage and chance giving his attackers another opening. Blood dripped at his feet in a soft *plop, plop*, steady droplets. He wasn't spurting blood like an artery had been hit, but the constant drip said blood loss was still a real concern for him.

His attackers must have come to the same conclusion because they stepped back, apparently content to wait for him to weaken so they could grab him and continue on with their original plan.

Karl glanced down and gulped. His arm wasn't gone, at least, but the missing chunk of muscle in his outer arm, just below his elbow, was going to make holding anything with his left hand difficult. Karl concentrated, focusing on getting the elbow to bend, but it only made his fingers shake and the pain to start throbbing in time with his fast-thudding heartbeats.

He was down to one arm—one knife—with five attackers and only minutes before he passed out—presuming the stabbing pain making him pant and wheeze didn't get him before the blood loss did. The time for playing was long over.

Karl called on his magic, letting the red light shine down his good arm and coat the knife. Moving was out of the question, so he couldn't stab them with the knife to use his magic like most users of red magic did, but he was Karl Musen, baker *and* spy. He wasn't most magic users. Karl slashed the knife horizontally through the air and a red ribbon erupted in the blade's wake before flying at the attackers with deadly aim.

The light was weaker than usual, fluctuating in a way Karl hadn't seen since his training days. Still, where it hit caused damage. Rot and decay didn't need much more than a touch to hurt. Three of the attackers let out screams and fell to the floor—one dead and the other two writhing in pain.

Two on one now. Karl bit his lip as his knees failed, and he dropped to the floor, the impact jarring his arm. He saw white, and then stars, and found he was slumped against the wall when awareness returned enough for him to notice. Blood dripped down his chin—blood he couldn't afford to lose. There might be only two attackers here, but the old lady was gone, and there was no telling what reinforcements she was getting. If Karl was going to survive this, he had to conserve enough energy to get out of the shop and find help, fast.

The edges of his vision were gray, the hand holding the knife shaking, but he stabbed forward once more, releasing a jet of red light at one of his attackers. But he was too slow, the light sluggish, and the woman simply grinned as she casually stepped out of the way.

The man hissed something—a literal hiss, his human-shaped tongue slithering out from between his lips as he spoke—and the woman grinned and said something in return. Her reply used regular words, but they made no sense to Karl. A knife dropped to the floor in front of him, and Karl blinked at it for a long second before realizing he wasn't holding it any longer. The woman strode forward, swaggering and smirking. Karl flicked his fingers at her, red magic flaring through the air, like the leftover glitter that had somehow still appeared two weeks after the school craft project Emily had inexplicably completed in Karl's dorm room. The woman dodged again and laughed, saying something else that didn't make any sense. She was a blurry figure, looming over Karl's slumped form, yet somehow the gleam of her sharp teeth was still perfectly visible.

Karl fought not to close his eyes, fought not to succumb, but body and brain were not in agreement. He was cold, shivering cold, and the gray in the corners of his vision was taking over. A crashing sound, like wood breaking violently, was the only sound Karl heard as his head hit the floor and blackness overtook him.

*

"GET A HEALER!"

Warmth, not from a blanket, but from strong arms, surrounded him. *Jolting up and down—too violent for a human's movements, so am I on a horse?*

"Bring him here!" Soothing magic filled his veins, overtaking even the warmth of those arms, and finally even those vague impressions faded into true sleep.

Chapter Twenty

THE CEILING WAS white. Karl contemplated that whiteness for a long while, studying the lines left in the paint from the brush and the shadows cast from some nearby light source. Then he closed his eyes again and slept.

When he reopened his eyes, the ceiling was still white, but the shadows were different. Longer, as if quite a lot of time had passed and the setting sun—or maybe rising sun, for all Karl knew—was low on the horizon. He could turn his head to look and see if there was a window and if his hunch was right, but even just the thought was too much effort, and he slid back into sleep.

Waking a third time was no different to the first two. The white ceiling and shadows were all still the same. Karl thought for a moment, and when that effort didn't knock him out, he slowly turned his head. One narrow window was set into the white wall parallel to the bed he was lying in.

The shade was up, letting in natural light. Having a window and a proper bed was important, but midway through Karl's struggle to remember why, he fell asleep yet again.

Thankfully, when he woke the fourth time, Karl did remember. Having a window and a comfortable bed meant he wasn't locked up in a cell somewhere in Yari, awaiting the same gruesome fate that had almost taken Ama's life. It also meant he had somehow survived. Karl didn't want to fall asleep again, so he resisted the urge to turn his head away from the window to look around at what he assumed was a healing ward somewhere.

Since he had survived, that must mean Braxton had noticed something and come to his rescue. Or maybe Ama had noticed. Karl wanted to know who—he was honestly secretly hoping it was Ama who came to save him—but he also really wanted to know how. What had he missed before the apple fiasco that could have alerted him? He was supposed to be Braxton's great spy—not as good as Ama, but still one of the best—and he had missed this trap until after it had already been sprung.

The creak of old hinges alerted Karl the door was opening and thankfully knocked him out of his useless, spiraling thoughts. He automatically turned his head to look, only belatedly remembering he hadn't wanted any extra exertion that might send him straight back to sleep. But he let out a relived breath to see Alina walking over to his bedside.

"You gave us quite the scare, Karl," she said, frowning at him. "Luckily, the healer here in the district housing many noble families is competent. He was able to restart your heart and stop the bleeding after Ama rushed you here."

So it was Ama who found him. Karl started to smile, but then the rest of her explanation filtered through.

"My heart?" he asked, his voice a mere croak of breathy weakness and disuse.

Alina nodded, still frowning severely at him. "You were technically dead when Healer Grigori started working on you. Luckily, not for very long, though, since Ama got you here in minutes, so you shouldn't have any permanent damage from that. They called me in to aid with the surgery for your arm, although I was already on my way when news of what happened reached the palace."

"My arm..." Karl trailed off, tilting his head again to look down at his left arm. The blanket covered him completely, so he couldn't see anything, but he also couldn't feel anything.

"Oh, yes. I shut off the pain receptors in your shoulder." She pulled the blanket back, revealing thick white bandages covering his entire arm. "You were in too much pain for regular painkillers, and this way you wouldn't be able to move your arm and reinjure yourself." Alina patted him on the shoulder, well above the bandages, and then touched the back of his left hand, below the bandages. Her touch on his shoulder was firm, but comforting, but he couldn't feel her fingers on his hand at all. "I'll confer with healer Grigori first, but now that you're awake and we don't have to worry about you thrashing in your sleep, I don't see why we can't manage your pain with painkillers." She started unraveling the bandages, careful not to move his arm too much in the process. Watching her touch him, but not feel any of it, was the oddest sensation Karl had ever experienced.

Once the bandages were removed, he was able to at least look at what had become of his arm.

"I'm not going to be able to knead bread, am I?" Karl asked, hoping she interpreted the choked note in his voice from his looking at the mess.

A four inch area of his arm, just below the elbow, was encased in a giant black scab, crusty and flaky with old blood. The scab filled a divot where his flesh had been carved out completely.

"That depends entirely on you, my dear." she replied. Her hands glowed green and a moment later the scab began to glow green as well. Usually healing magic was soothing, but Karl still had the disconcerting sense of not feeling what he could *see* she was doing.

"What do you mean?" he asked, having zero idea of what she was talking about. There was an apple-sized chunk of flesh missing from an arm he couldn't move or feel. Of course, he wasn't going to be baking again. Karl clenched his right hand into a fist, trying to suppress the ache in his chest that wanted to erupt from his eyes as tears.

Alina focused on her healing, but she glanced up at him through her lashes and her frown reappeared. "To be honest, you got lucky. They carved you up good, but the spot they took was mostly muscle. Also, you know I'm not bragging when I say I'm the best healer in the country. Especially what with you silly princes giving me all kinds of practice these last few years. While Grigori kept you from bleeding out and your heart from stopping again, I was able to start the process of rebuilding the tendons and ligaments that were cut, get the bone they sliced to begin knitting, and begin returning your arm to the right shape. It's taken me nearly every waking moment of these last three weeks, but all I can really do from here on is provide some magical encouragement and support. You are the one who's going to have to put in the work. A few years of therapy are in your future, slowly stretching the tendons and ligaments out so you have full use of your arm and rebuilding muscle. But if you put in the work, one day, you should have full use of the arm again. Although, your days as a high stakes spy are likely over."

Karl snorted out a laugh. "I think my life was heading in that direction before this anyway. I've found lately all I want is a peaceful life to enjoy having a bakery and figuring out what I'm doing with inheriting a noble title. No more sneaking around in the shadows."

"Which means the chances of you ever ending up in my care again are slim." Alina gave him a look, but it only made him laugh more. Instead of commenting, she retracted her magic and pulled out some ointment to rub over the scab. When she was done, she rewrapped his arm in fresh bandages. "I'll confer with Grigori about when to remove the block on your arm. Are you up for some visitors?" she asked.

"I might fall asleep mid-word, but yes, please," Karl replied, already looking toward the door in the hopes that Ama was out there.

"No, we don't need to keep you sedated any longer. You're healing, so you'll be tired, but not as much as you were before. I'll tell them to come in." She left the door open as she left, and a moment later Char and Fen walked in, Braxton and Caro a step behind them.

"This wasn't what I expected to come home to, you know," Fen said with a cheeky smile. "Someone"—he shot Braxton a look—"said they had the issue with Yaroi under control when I left."

"It was under control. Not my fault they snuck an old lady in. She wasn't exactly your typical spy."

"Did you catch her?" Karl asked, interrupting their brotherly snarking.

Braxton puffed out his chest, but Fen cut in before he could speak. "Shairon did most of the work." Shairon was Braxton and Fen's older sister. She also did something military in nature for work, although Karl had never been sure what. She wasn't a commander like Fen or like Braxton's rank, nor did she do the clandestine work Braxton specialized in, but she was as involved with the military as they were.

"She only did the overt work, thank you very much!" Braxton added. "Listen, Karl. I'm so sorry you got caught up in this. I had the two groups of fighters Yaroi thought they'd successfully snuck into the city completely encircled, but I missed the little old lady living quietly above the bakery with eight people she called her grandchildren—but who turned out to the eight Yarokian thugs who hurt you. I only realized she was part of a plot early the same morning you were attacked, when I got a report one of the groups of soldiers was on the move. I thought they were headed to your house, so I sent men there. Unfortunately, or maybe fortunately, they arrived just in time for Ama to steal one of their horses and whisk you away to the nearest healer."

So Alina was right, and Ama had found him. "Where is Ama?" Karl asked.

"He's giving us time with you," Char replied, giving Karl a gentle smile. "I believe he's waiting for us to leave so he can have some private time with you," Char added with a wink.

"Char and I weren't gone that long," Fen added. "Yet in that short time you've managed to get yourself seriously injured and get yourself a paramour. No more crazy spy missions for you!"

"That depends on whether the situation with Yaroi is resolved," Karl replied, his leading statement half joking and half curious. Plus, while he appreciated the chance to see his family, getting them to finish telling him everything they wanted to say would allow him to see Ama sooner.

"Of course, it's resolved!" Braxton puffed out his chest again in a "what do you take me for?" move. "Both groups were apprehended, including the old lady. Prince Lyric helped write the strongly worded missive we sent to Yaroi about it all. I suspect Toval will have some difficulties with trade deals with Yaroi and some extra tariffs on our goods traveling through the Eiroi Strait, but it's reached a point where they really can't continue trying to kill you both. At least, while you're within the borders of Toval and Namin. I suggest you settle into the life of a baron, maybe have some kids with Ama—"

"And I'll finish refurbishing that lovely bakery, where you almost died, for when you're allowed to leave Healer Grigori's clinic. You'll be able to bake all you want too," Char added, shamelessly cutting Braxton off.

"So don't worry about anything," Fen finished. "Focus on healing. Okay?"

Karl nodded slowly. "I can do that. Thanks for coming out here."

"Of course," Char replied. "Although I'm not sure Healer Grigori realized just who had nearly kicked down his door when Ama brought you here until we showed up the first time. Oh, Emily and Shan were here this morning. They both had work this afternoon, so they'll come see you again tomorrow." He gripped Karl's good shoulder, his touch the comfort it had always been, from the first day Char had taken one look at a homeless waif who didn't even know how to shower. "We'll try to stop by too. Get some rest. We'll send Ama in on our way out."

Fen also patted Karl on his good shoulder. Braxton gave him a nod that said he had done well. Caro smiled and waved. And then they were gone. Not even a minute later, Casmir walked into the room. His back was straight and his bearing nothing short of royal. Even though he was only wearing black pants and a gray shirt, he was clearly a noble of the highest level. Casmir closed the door and between one breath and the next, he tucked away the persona of Prince Casmir. Ama didn't slouch, but his bearing was more relaxed and casual. He was letting Karl see the real him, not the façade of Casmir, nor the old façade that was Ama the spy. This was more a Cama, or an Asmir, a combination of both, yet neither at the same time. Now he showed his real self, bared in a way Karl knew no one else except Karl had seen in a very long time.

He took Karl's breath away every time he revealed himself, and all Karl could do was marvel as Ama walked closer. Ama's eyes were blazing with emotion—joy when he saw Karl was awake and looking at him, but also something more, deeper, as if Ama was releasing an emotion kept as hidden as his real personality.

"I guess it was your turn to save me," Karl said when Ama reached his bedside, desperate to say something in response to the power in Ama's gaze.

Ama laughed. "I think we should both agree to not make a habit out of needing desperate rescues." His smile faded as he looked at Karl, taking in the thick bandages around his arm. "I got complacent. I'm sorry I let this happen to you."

Karl shook his head. "This was no one's fault except Yaroi's. I didn't notice anything was wrong until the very last moment, same as Braxton. If we didn't know, how could you? Please don't blame yourself for any of this."

Ama let out a slow sigh, his shoulders slumping. "You've been kept unconscious for three weeks, and I've spent this entire time trying to figure out what clue I missed. If it hadn't been for Leslie mentioning offhand that the old lady who ran the bakery died, I wouldn't have gotten there in time to save you."

"But you did," Karl replied, his tone insistent. He held out his good hand and waited for Ama to take it. "When the clues finally did come together, you did exactly what I needed. You have to stop blaming yourself for the impossible and, instead, praise yourself for the good you actually accomplished."

"I can't—" Ama cut himself off, taking in a shaky breath and gripping Karl's hand with both of his. The intensity in Ama's eyes returned full force, those emotions bursting out, like biting into a berry in a freshly baked muffin—a sweet explosion that Karl desperately wanted more of.

"I can't lose you," Ama continued, his voice choked with the same feelings. "I know we've only known each other for a few short months, but from the very first moment we met, when you risked yourself to save me, even though I was basically dead, I knew I was going to fall in love with you."

Karl swallowed a gasp, his eyes tearing as Ama said the exact words inside his own heart. Words Karl had never thought he would have the opportunity to say because Ama was a prince and so very special. Why would he want a street rat like Karl? And yet, the intensity in Ama's eyes and the strength in his grip said this wasn't a joke.

"The second I cut you down, back in Yari, you led your own rescue. You were bleeding and in so much pain, but you still smiled and took charge. That bravery was astounding to me," Karl admitted. "And then you took that bravery a step further and revealed your true identity. I've never been in love before, but I think I realized I was developing feelings for you when you started to fall ill and I felt so helpless to do anything."

"That's how I've felt these last three weeks," Ama added. "Helpless. Wishing you would open your eyes so I had the chance to tell you the truth.

I love you, Karl. Would you have me?"

Karl's answer flew from his mouth, no thought necessary. "Yes! Of course, yes!"

Karl wished his other arm would work because all he wanted was to pull Ama into a hug. At least he had one good hand, so he squeezed Ama's hand in return. Ama bent and pressed a kiss to Karl's knuckles. He glanced up at Karl through damp lashes and smiled. Karl tugged on their joined hands and Ama obeyed, leaning closer until their lips met.

The mere touch was like licking a spoon full of hot honey, perfectly sweet, but with a kick of chili behind it that served to make Karl crave more. Karl wanted to devour the entire pot, licking each drip like the indolent prince he was supposed to be. Yet, he was prone on his back with Ama so very carefully leaning over him.

There would be other opportunities—a whole lifetime together to explore the promise in their kiss—so Karl didn't protest when Ama slowly pulled away. Alina said Karl's recovery was entirely dependent on the work he put in. Well, the look in Ama's eyes full of want was only echoed in the desire churning inside Karl. He wanted Ama in a physical sense, but Karl also wanted that promised long future hand in hand with Ama. Karl would put in whatever work Alina asked of him to ensure he had the hands to do that with.

Karl knew that together, they would both be all right.

Epilogue

AMA

Ama walked down the aisle first. Being a prince of two nations gave him higher rank, even with Karl's convoluted connection to nobility. Quasi-prince and baron did not trump double prince. Which meant Ama walked down the aisle first and then had the pleasure of watching Karl take his turn. Karl walked slowly, practically glowing in his white suit with all his military pins on his chest. A diadem crowned his brow, the silver a perfect match to the buttons on his jacket. Ama wore nearly the same outfit, but his embellishments were in gold, and he wore an actual crown—albeit a small one suitable for a royal prince not in line for inheritance of the throne. The only other difference in their outfits was the white sling holding Karl's left arm immobile. He could use it for day-to-day tasks now, thanks to hours upon hours of physical therapy over the last six months, but the healers didn't want him to use it fully just yet and his arm definitely wasn't back to anywhere close to full strength. Either way, Karl was absolutely beautiful, and Ama could watch him walk down the aisle every day for the rest of his life. In fact, that was the entire wonderous point of the day.

"His Royal Highness, Prince Casmir Sventoval. Lord Karlow Musen Whist, the Baron Whistfield," Ayer called when Karl stopped walking at Ama's side. Karl smiled at Ama, joy and excitement in every movement, then held out his right hand. Ama smiled back, hoping his own happiness was just as evident, took Karl's hand in his left, and they both turned to look at Ayer.

Crown Prince Ayer had asked them if he might officiate. Primarily because he was Karl's uncle, but also to show his support for them. Politically, his officiating sent a message informing others Ayer had no coup or usurping fears from them, individually or because of their union.

"We come together today to bring these two august persons together in the bonds of matrimony," Ayer continued, his voice echoing through the room and over the heads of the dozens of people in attendance. "Your Highnesses?" he added, bowing to two people behind Ama and Karl.

Queen Carmillian stepped up first, allowed the honor as a visiting dignitary. One of the main reasons they'd needed to wait six whole months to hold the wedding—aside from giving Karl enough time to heal—was to complete all the diplomatic wrangling required to allow the Queen of Namin to visit Etoval. Aunt Millie was wearing the colors of state, the brilliant blue and gold of Namin. She strode forward with a delicate swish of skirts to place her hands on both their shoulders.

"Namin welcomes this union and this opportunity to unite our kingdoms with even stronger bonds!" She pressed a kiss to their cheeks, in turn, before moving around Ama to stand at his side.

King Aurelius stepped up next, his suit in the darker gold and gray of Toval. "Toval welcomes this union between my nearly adopted grandson and my nephew. Through their marriage, we welcome the chance to finally, fully welcome Prince Karlow Musen-Val Whist into our family, even if it was by marriage rather than adoption." He copied Aunt Millie by kissing them both on the cheek, either oblivious to Karl's dropped jaw and the exclamations of surprise from some of the audience for naming him a prince, or more likely, not caring. He smiled at them both, then stepped aside, returning to his seat in the first row. Fen and Char took his place, copying Aunt Millie by standing to Karl's side.

"Casmir, do you take this man as he is, who when bereft of fancy titles of state is a simple man named Karl?"

Karl was beaming, his eyes shimmering with pooling tears of happiness. He had never looked more beautiful. From the first moment Ama had ever seen Karl—himself half delirious with pain, mostly dead, and hanging off the saltire cross—something had drawn him in and made him want to know more about Karl. Every moment since had only cemented that draw because Karl was everything Ama had never before dared dream he might have. Love, happiness, a person who meant more than anything else in his life—that was Karl to Ama.

"I do," Ama said with no hesitation and absolute conviction in every fiber of his being. Karl was the man Ama wanted to marry, and he was taking this opportunity to announce it for everyone to hear.

"Do you, Karlow, take this man as he is, who when bereft of fancy titles of state is a simple man named Cas?"

Ama's smile was as wide as Karl's, and he had to blink to keep his swimming vision clear so he could see the way Karl's eyes crinkled at the corners as his smile grew just before he also answered, "I do."

"Then, with the power vested in me as the heir apparent of these lands, surrounded by the king and queen who support you, and sealed by the parents who raised you, I now pronounce you married!" Ayer stepped back and bowed with a flourish. When he straightened again, he called out the last line, "You may now kiss your husband!"

Ama's hands were steady as he reached out to cup Karl's cheeks. He didn't know why he assumed they would be shaking, but he was certain that this moment was the best of his entire life, and he wanted it to be perfect for them both. Karl tilted his head as Ama bent forward, and their lips touched, firm and dry, a chaste kiss giving consideration that they were in public. Yet Ama's eyes slid closed, and he pressed closer, glad when Karl's good arm wrapped around his shoulders since his knees were barely holding him up.

He didn't want to pull away, but Ama also knew there would be time later for some of the more carnal promises in that kiss. Still, even as the kiss ended, he couldn't completely step away just yet. He had to press his forehead to Karl's, staring into those amazing golden-brown eyes and seeing love looking back. Only when Karl crinkled his nose in laughter did the spell break. Ama moved just far enough away to clasp hands with Karl, but he was absolutely certain there would be plenty of time later to rekindle that moment. They had forever together to look forward to, after all.

*

BRAXTON

"My two best spies just retired," Braxton groaned, muffling his words in

Caro's jacketed shoulder. They were sitting in the front row with the rest of the family, but Braxton needn't have bothered muffling at all since the cheering and clapping as Ama and Karl finally turned to look at the audience was practically deafening.

Caro snickered. "I think those two would get really bored without you giving them something to do. Maybe nothing as dangerous as the Yaroi mission again, but I'm sure you'll have something fun for them to tackle soon enough."

"Presuming we can drag Karl out of that little bakery Char bought him near his city house," Braxton tacked on. "Kid's still as mad about food as his father, even with a bum arm."

Caro laughed again. "The arm is healing. He might not be as good with a blade or at kneading bread with that arm as he was before, but knowing Karl, that won't stop him. Now hush, I want to enjoy this."

Braxton settled back into his seat, stifling his own chuckle. Ama and Karl might be facing the crowd, but the way they both kept stealing glances with each other said they really only wanted to be together right now. They reminded Braxton of his own wedding to Caro.

Queen Carmillian hadn't been able to come to theirs since Namin was in too much disarray at the time, but she had sent her daughter to stand in for Caro's family. Caro had Alina to stand at his side, but also having blood family in addition to his dearest friend had really made Caro happy. And yet, there had been that moment standing together, as King Aurelius declared them married, when all concerns had simply fallen away. Only he and Caro had stood there, the rest of the world gone, the two reveling in being together and knowing it was for forever. Braxton was certain that was exactly what Ama and Karl were experiencing right at this moment.

The two newlyweds continued to hold hands as they started walking back down the aisle together. Braxton stood along with everyone else, still clapping, as the room honored the couple's milestone. Only once they walked through the doors at the far end did the clapping stop as the rest of the attendees began milling around while they waited for cocktail hour to begin before the celebratory ball that evening.

"You know," Caro murmured into Braxton's ear as his hand slid into Braxton's to clasp him close. "You could always train some new spies."

Braxton squeezed Caro's hand, following his gaze to where Shan and Lyric were standing together against one wall. The two of them were a couple and had announced their relationship to the family, but they could never get married. Yaroi might be willing to overlook one of their royal princes choosing to stay in Toval, especially after the message Toval sent after the near-fiasco that almost killed Karl, but they wouldn't overlook Lyric marrying into the royal family, even if Shan was only a quasi-royal like Karl had been. Yaroi would invade if anyone even thought the word marriage for too long. But Shan and Lyric seemed happy together anyway.

And, as usual, Caro was correct that they would make excellent spies. As a very skilled sous chef, Shan's abilities would open doors into places similar to how Karl had used his baking skills in the past. Lyric could literally fly, and there was no telling what else he could do.

"It's an interesting thought," Braxton replied. He looked at Caro and snuck a quick peck of a kiss. "But not today. Let's celebrate Ama and Karl today and maybe recreate certain parts of our own wedding night later." Braxton let his mischievous grin indicate to Caro exactly which portions of that night he meant. "I'll think about spies again tomorrow."

Caro's answering smirk said he was definitely on board with Braxton's plans. "Then I expect you to dance with me tonight. You have to woo me."

"But I hate dancing," Braxton groaned, his tone slightly whiny and only half-joking.

"But you love me," Caro added pointedly.

"Yes, I do," Braxton answered easily. He lifted their clasped hands and pressed a kiss to the back of Caro's, feathering his lips over where their fingers were intertwined.

"I love you too," Caro replied, his tone gruff, but then he brightened. "Which is why a dance or two won't hurt you. Besides, I know that you know you actually enjoy dancing with me."

Braxton tried to hold onto his morose façade, but the laugh escaped before he could stop it. "Only when I'm with you, Caro."

They were pulled into the throng of people heading en masse toward the social hall where the cocktail hour was being held as the next stage of Ama and Karl's wedding began. The promise of forever Braxton and Caro had made at their own wedding all those years ago might mean Braxton had to dance at events like these, but as usual, Caro was right again. Braxton would never turn down a chance to hold Caro close.

Because together forever was definitely worth it.

*

FEN

Locating Char amid the throngs of guests at the ball was as easy for Fen as always. Char was by the banquet table, checking out the quality of the food. Fen took a wide path around the dance floor where Braxton was getting carted around by Caro, and cut through the tables where many people were sitting and enjoying the lavish feast. Char wasn't eating anything when Fen finally reached his side—well, of course he wasn't. The man could look at a pastry crust and immediately tell if it was lacking even a teaspoon of butter; he didn't need to taste something to know whether it was well-made.

"So, how much of this did you help cook?" Fen asked. He slid an arm around Char's waist and bent close so Char could hear him, which also let him sneak a quick kiss.

"Terrance blocked me from the kitchen, remember?" Char replied. He frowned for a brief moment, but when Fen grabbed another kiss, the frown melted away. "Stop that! Anyway, because of that, I wasn't able to help out. Um…much…"

Fen laughed. "You snuck in when your cousin was out, didn't you?" Char's cousin Terrance was admittedly better at paperwork and ordering than actually cooking, but he was an Aba-Musen, same as Char, so his ability to nullify poison was invaluable in the castle. However, Char made it a habit to stop by the castle kitchens when he was staying over, so even if Terrance wasn't improving, the other kitchen chefs were learning a ton. The quality of the food had improved significantly since Char had joined them.

"I may have done that," Char said, hedging. "But Terrance let me help with the wedding cake, so I didn't always have to sneak."

Terrance had Char help with the wedding cake because serving sub-par wedding cake to someone as incredibly talented as Karl would have been an unrecoverable insult. Of everyone in the country of Toval, only Char was better at baking cake than Karl, but an average tongue wouldn't be able to taste the difference between Char's and Karl's baked creations.

"Well, I will definitely make certain to have a slice of cake once it's served." Fen tugged gently with the arm he had wrapped around Char.

"Until then, come dance with me. We can't have Braxton be the only one grimacing and trying not to step on people's feet out there."

"Hey! My dancing has gotten a lot better, thank you very much," Char replied. He didn't resist when Fen tugged a second time, joining Fen in an open spot on the floor and picking up the steps of the current song midway. They twirled together, hands clasped, bodies close, and Fen took in every movement of the beautiful man he loved.

"Who knew not killing you that day in the forest would lead to all this," Fen murmured. Char tilted his head upward and to the side, as if to say "what? I couldn't hear you." Fen just laughed and stole yet another kiss.

They spun around Braxton and Caro, who had only met and fallen in love because Char had intervened at the lake. They passed by Queen Carmillian, apparently holding court at a table adjacent to the dance floor and looking regal. And finally, as the song came to a close and they slowed, they turned to look at where Karl and Casmir sat close together, practically cuddling, at the newlywed's table. Adopting Karl had been troublesome, but the good sort of troublesome. Now they had added Casmir to their family, which felt completely right.

Even with all the battles they fought and the hardships they endured, they had all somehow found peace and love. The orchestra started playing a new song. Fen looked away from the newlyweds to focus on his own husband, taking Char into his arms and whisking him away, off into the remainder of a perfect evening and the rest of their lives together.

Recipes

Mama Poma's (not poisoned) Apple Bread

INGREDIENTS

    1 ½ c. all-purpose flour

    ½ tsp. baking soda

    ¼ tsp. baking powder

    1 ¼ tsp. cinnamon

    ½ tsp. ground ginger

    ½ tsp. salt

    ½ c. plus 1 tbsp. sugar

    ½ c. brown sugar

    2 large eggs

    1 tsp. vanilla

    ½ c. vegetable oil

    1 ½ c. chopped Granny Smith apples with peel, seeds, and core removed (approximately 3 apples total, chopped into fine brunoise size)

    1 tsp. butter, for greasing pan (or, alternatively, coat pan in spray oil)

DIRECTIONS

1. Preheat oven to 350°. Butter or spray a 5 x 10 inch loaf pan.
2. In a medium bowl, whisk together flour, baking soda, baking powder, cinnamon, ginger, and salt.
3. In a large bowl, beat eggs for 30 seconds with a fork (or whisk). Add vanilla, ½ c. sugar, and brown sugar. Stir until combined. Whisk in vegetable oil.
4. Add flour mixture to wet ingredients in two additions, mixing until just combined.
5. Stir chopped apples into batter until evenly distributed.
6. Pour batter into prepared loaf pan and sprinkle top with remaining tablespoon of sugar.
7. Bake about 40 minutes, until golden and cake tester comes out clean.

About the Author

When Mell Eight was in high school, she discovered dragons. Beautiful, wondrous creatures that took her on epic adventures both to faraway lands and on journeys of the heart. Mell wanted to create dragons of her own, so she put pen to paper. Mell Eight is now known for her own soaring dragons, as well as for other wonderful characters dancing across the pages of her books. While she mostly writes paranormal or fantasy stories, she has been seen exploring the real world once or twice.

Facebook

www.facebook.com/MellEightFiction

Twitter

www.x.com/MellEight

Website

www.melleightfiction.weebly.com

BlueSky

bsky.app/profile/melleight.bsky.social

Instagram

www.instagram.com/mell_eight

Threads

www.threads.net/mell_eight

Other NineStar books by this author

Princes of Toval Series

The Chef

The Prince

Witch's Circle Series

Coven

Hunter

Witch

Ge-Mi Series

Ge-Mi, Part One

Ge-Mi, Part Two

Oracle Series

The Oracle's Flame

The Oracle's Hatchling

The Oracle's Golem

The Oracle's Sprite

The Oracle's Prophecy

The Oracle's Current

Supernatural Consultant Series

Dragon Consultant

Dragon Deception

Dragon Dilemma

Dragon Detective

Dragon Soldier

Dragon Adventures

Dragon Lesson

Out of Underhill Series

Kelpie Blue

If a Butterfly Don't Fly

Magnified Series

Magnified

Justified

Dragon's Hoard Series

Finding the Wolf

Breaking the Shackles

Stealing the Dragon

Melting the Ice Witch

Road to… Series

Road to Revenge

Road to Home

Wizard Wars Series

Ground of Insurrection

Ground of Resurrection

Standalone Books

Elemental Ride

A Little Fairy Dust

Wounded Alpha

The Coup and the Prince

Space Stars

Water's Price

Twin Elements

Soul Bond

Gifting a Dragon's Heart

www.ninestarpress.com

www.facebook.com/ninestarpress

www.facebook.com/groups/NineStarNiche

www.twitter.com/ninestarpress

www.instagram.com/ninestarpress

bsky.app/profile/ninestarpress.bsky.social

www.threads.net/@ninestarpress

www.ingramcontent.com/pod-product-compliance
Lightning Source LLC
Chambersburg PA
CBHW070531100726
47907CB00004B/1065